FYNN

Dennis Lightfoot

With thanks to…

Lunette Puckridge for the cover image.

Aileen Pluker for editing.

Mary G for publishing assistance.

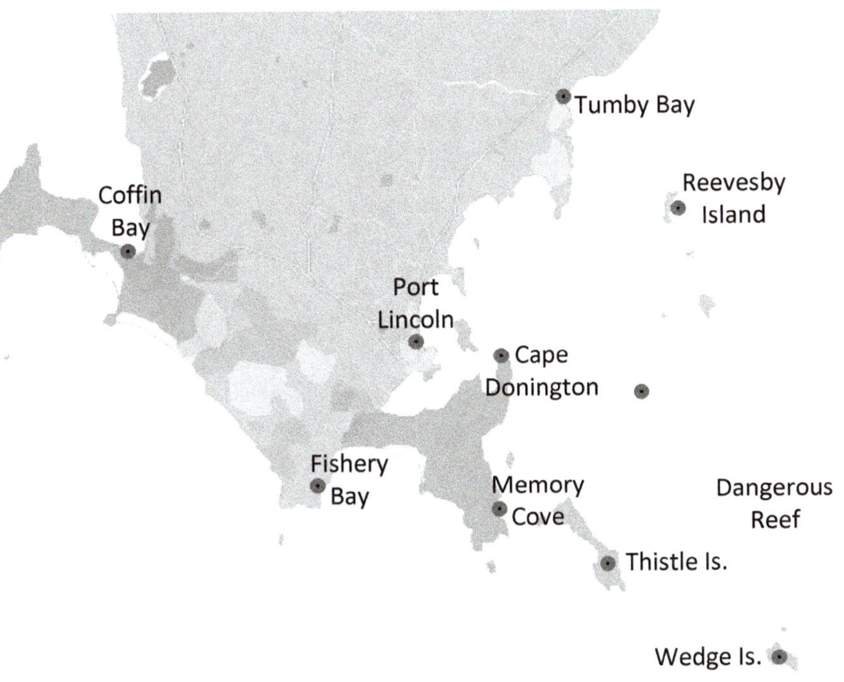

Google Map data ©2021

FYNN

Mark 'Flippers' Britcher spent every day possible, either in, on or under the water. Both his father and grandfather were Port Lincoln tuna fishermen and 'Flippers' connection with the sea began at an early age. Young Mark often accompanied his father on board the family fishing boat to watch the catch being off-loaded.

A well-tanned and athletic Helen Wilson likewise had a passion for the sea. Her father was also in the local fishing industry, operating his lobster vessel out of the Lincoln Marina.

Throughout the summer and autumn months Miss Wilson would swim each morning as part of her keeping fit routine. In the colder months Helen preferred to keep her body in shape by jogging along the many bush tracks that hemmed the three bays that were located close to the town.

With parents in a similar business and residing in the same city it may have been expected that Mark and she would have known each other. This was not the case. Her first meeting with Mark, albeit very briefly, happened one day when she was swimming.

Summer time on Eyre Peninsula! – Another glorious mid-January, Mediterranean type of day on Boston Harbour! The temperature hovered around a balmy 32 degrees. The enticing turquoise water of the bay, bustled with activity – yachting, paddle-boarding and swimming.

Miss Wilson was an excellent swimmer who loved the challenge of swimming long distances. On days such as this she could not resist taking an afternoon dip in addition to her regular morning splash. Shelley Beach was her favourite swimming spot – that is where Helen chose to swim that particular day. Leaving her towel and sandals on the sand she had swum out beyond the blue-line to the deeper water 200 metres out from shore to where a mooring-buoy was positioned. While holding onto a floating rope attached to the buoy Helen was lazily treading water while considering which direction she would continue her swim. Unexpectedly a large dark shape swam beneath her.

SHARK! Flashed across her mind. Before she had time to react or panic, a goggled faced diver in a black wet-suit surfaced behind her.

"You scared the bloody hell out of me! For a moment I thought a shark was going to have me for lunch!" she blurted out toward whoever it was clad in neoprene.

"Sorry, I didn't mean to" the scuba diver spluttered as he removed his mouthpiece.

"Just checking the mooring chain was not tangled – bringing my boat around tomorrow and going to tie-up here." Then replaced his mouth-piece, with a quick duck-dive slipped back under the water as fast as he had appeared.

Expecting the mystery diver to resurface, Helen held the mooring rope for several minutes, but he had vanished as mysteriously as he had arrived. "Who was that strange man and where did he go?" Helen thought. Having been slightly rattled by the encounter she swam back to shore to sun-bake rather than swim any further.

Next day the heat continued and the water was again totally irresistible. Helen returned to Shelley Beach. Once more she swam out to the mooring buoy not giving thought to the previous day brief experience, simply enjoying the pleasure of being in the water. She had been there for several minutes lazily floating on her back whilst holding on to the same rope. Her attention was occupied watching some children attempting to upright their overturned canoe.

"Look out," yelled a voice from behind her. Instantly turning around she was surprised to see the hull of a boat silently looming toward the mooring, on a collision course with her body. It was too late for her to move away. All she could do to dodge the incoming vessel was to position her feet towards the approaching hull. This action then propelled her forward almost jamming her between the boat and buoy. A long aluminium shaft of a boat hook aimed at the mooring almost hit her as it was thrust forward as it reached to collect the attached rope.

Being almost run down by a boat was one thing, then having a gaff shaft thrust at her body, immediately enraged Helen. When she saw the perpetrator on the other end of the pole was none other than the diver she had encountered the previous day she exploded.

"It's bloody you again, are you deliberately trying to scare the life out of me or simply kill me," she angrily yelled as she back paddled away from the vessel.

"Don't get your tits in a tangle," was his unexpected rude reply. "Come aboard so I can apologise. Swim around to the stern – you can get up on the ladder," he then repentantly added.

Out of sheer curiosity the rather miffed Miss Wilson swam

to the back of the boat and clambered up the stainless steel ladder. As she climbed over the stern guard-rail Helen saw what the mystery man looked like without his diving gear. His hair was sandy-blonde probably better described as sun-bleached. Not over tall, but carrying himself in such a manner that it emphasised his broad shoulders, muscular legs and strong arms.

Helen liked what she saw. When her feet were firmly on the deck she blasted him again, "You might have killed me," she stated, with obvious annoyance.

"I'm sorry if you thought I was going to run you over. I haven't finished servicing the motor. Only had sail power to get the boat here. Boats don't have brakes and I was going to use the mooring to stop her. She slips through the water very quietly – doesn't she?" The young man said as he took a lingering look at her.

"Quiet? Don't you mean silent? It was just like yesterday. You sneak up then suddenly appear, scaring the hell out of me. Are you going to disappear again today?" Helen retorted.

"I am sorry about that too," he nonchalantly replied then introduced himself.

"I'm Mark, but most people call me 'Flippers' and you are on board the *Amethyst* the jewel of the sea – my pride and joy."

Helen's eyes surveyed the layout of the boat. On its large deck area she noted two tubs of diving equipment and several bins of ropes all neatly coiled, stacked forward of the helm.

"Not sure if I am pleased to meet you, I'm Helen, and most people call me Helen," she said haughtily as she walked towards the cabin to have a look inside.

Helen's Dad Laurie was a lobster fisherman and had taught her about boats. She noticed the tidiness and how well the

Amethyst was laid out. "Immaculate," she muttered quietly to herself while noting the beautiful timber work everywhere, a very roomy galley. On the Port side was a table that was flanked by leather upholstered seats. On the Starboard side was a chart alcove at the foot of the steps. Radios and electronic navigation equipment were built into the woodwork above the chart table. More forward a companion-way led to other cabins but was shut. 'Probably sleeping quarters and probably just as neat' she guessed.

"It's a very nice boat. Have you had it long?"

"It was my fathers. He built her and before he died, made me promise to keep her and look after it just as he did – I'm keeping that promise."

After Helen had forgiven Mark for his insensitive actions, those first impromptu encounters became the start of a growing friendship. Both had a similar background and a natural love of the sea. Within three months their companionship turned to romance and they began dating. Many romantic weekends were spent aboard Mark's boat, sometimes with a bit of sailing and diving thrown into the mix of their 'other' onboard activities. After an amorous two-year engagement they married. The ceremony was held at the local Anglican Church, chosen by Mark as it was the closest one to the sea.

Mark's casual beach bum appearance contradicted that of him being a well-educated graduate with a Doctorate in the study of Cetacean species and now working as researcher for the University as a marine biologist. His work involved investigating the breeding cycle of the bottle-nosed dolphin (tursiops truncatus). Much of his time was spent at sea onboard the research vessel 'Pisces', following and recording the behaviour patterns of the in-shore Spencer Gulf dolphin population.

Helen worked as a data collector for the fishing industry. During the fishing season most of her days were aboard the fishing fleet vessels monitoring catch sizes and collecting serial numbers from tagged fish.

Mark had formed a connection with a local pod of Dolphin, but more-so with a pair that he had given the quaint names of Dick and Dora. The duo appeared bonded and Mark focused his attention principally on them, to study if, when and how the two dolphins would mate. Over a period of several months Mark had regular contact with the pair. Gradually he was able to get close enough to hand feed and touch them. He was aware that feeding them may cause problems of relying on his food, instead of hunting for their own. Therefore food was limited at first, to just a morsel each day to maintain being approachable.

All was going well with the research but Mark required more biological material to complete his studies. He needed to obtain blood and other samples to record any changes in hormone levels and body temperatures of his mammalian subjects, something that was not easily achievable at sea.

On the other side of the bay in an area sheltered by Boston Island a large sea-pen was fashioned from a disused pontoon and tuna ring net obtained from a nearby aquaculture farm. In this the dolphin could be held for a few months to allow Dick and Dora to become more confident with human contact. To lure them into their temporary home Mark began supplying more food each day until they followed him through a gap he had opened in a section of net.

When the pair were settled inside their temporary home

Mark would swim daily with his captives. Their trust in him grew quickly, now that he was the sole supplier of their nourishment. With extra fish as their reward, it took only a few days for Mark to teach the powerful 320kg 'Dick' and the smaller 280kg 'Dora,' to swim into the special catching net where he could handle them and gather the necessary samples for his studies. Dick relished the added attention but Dora was more reserved and took longer to accept any examinations.

Mark was extremely particular with his work, the same pride and meticulousness he took maintaining the *Amethyst*. Everything must be done to perfection. All samples taken from his aquatic subjects were labeled, recorded in a notebook and entered on his computer. Three spare vials of each sample taken were to be frozen for future study. There were no exceptions to this rule.

Helens' life with Mark encapsulated everything she had dreamed. The man she married was intelligent, handsome and incredibly fit. He came with an added bonus of being totally committed to her. They had a beautiful house, almost at the waters edge overlooking Shelley Beach and handily located within walking distance to Mark's workplace. Both had the occupations they had studied hard to achieve.

In addition to having the perfect husband, Helen had wonderful close friends especially Kerrie and Julie. Kerrie was her rock – a person with whom Helen could confide in and discuss her most intimate of thoughts. With Kerrie's understanding of health issues was second-to-none. She had studied Naturopathy and Natural Birthing and held a Diploma in both subjects. Julie was almost the opposite of both Kerrie and

Helen. Julie was what might be described as being 'off with the fairies' at times. Apart from her alternative style of life and thinking, her only desire was to paint and write poetry. Her artworks were marine-theme and dove-tailed well with Helen and Mark's love of the sea. Many of the shells and sea creatures featured in her artistic creations were supplied by Mark. Possibly the only bloke that fully understood Julie was her remnant from the hippy days, her 'out-there' boyfriend Peter, who usually dressed in batik printed shirts and wore leather sandals and completed his scruffy look with his long hair tied in a ponytail.

Yet despite having a nice house, good friends and an interesting career, Helen had deep within her a yearning, one that she could never quite explain.

Mark's best mates were Ian, a local doctor – and James, a fellow researcher at the Science Centre. It was usual practice for a bottle or two of the delightful local red wine to become empty on the nights they met, often sharing a meal at each other's home. The venue changed regularly, alternating turns between their houses. Helen treasured the nights that a dinner was held at their house. Julie and Kerrie would be invited as well to these gatherings. Breaking bread (as they called it) with her and Mark's friends present, made these evenings a pleasurable experience.

At one of those shared dinners Julie happily announced that she was three months pregnant and the baby was due in September. It was then Helen realised what was the missing factor from her life – a child of their own.

For the rest of that evening all discussions turned towards

babies. Helen who was never one to hold herself back said to Mark, "Let's start a family of our own, I'm young and fit and rearing to go, so why not?"

"Darling, if that's what you really want, I cannot see a reason for not starting one as soon as possible – what say we start tonight," came Marks smiling reply.

"Hip, hip, hooray for Helen and Flippers," the group laughingly cheered, then James jokingly added "any baby that you two have will probably be born with scales!"

That night, just as Mark was turning out the bedside light, Helen asked, "Did you really mean what you said about starting one now?"

"Sure, why not, "Mark replied, "You will make a wonderful mother and now would be a good time to start as I will be releasing the Dolphins soon and I will have plenty of time for you and a baby."

Several weeks had gone by when Kerrie and Julie came to enquire whether Helen had become pregnant.

"Don't know" was Helens reply to their question. "Have you done a test to see," Julie enquired.

"Nope," Helen giggled.

"Lucky for you I bought a test-kit with me today," Kerrie said.

"Now go to the bathroom and test yourself," Julie whispered into Helen's ear.

A few minute later Helen emerged "What's the result," both women asked simultaneously.

"Nothing doing," Helen said softly.

"Oh well – keep on trying – maybe on your next ovulation you will click," Kerrie said in her most medical voice.

Three months elapsed and Helen did regular checks to ascertain if she had yet conceived. Each test showed negative and Helen became more despondent with the thought of not starting a family. Mark noticed his wife was becoming less enthusiastic with the idea and in his usual thoroughness remarked. "Let us both see Doctor Ian to check if either of one has a problem and then we will know why it's not working."

Appointments were made to see the Doctor at his clinic. It was Helen who went first. Blood test, a general check and an ultrasound to check her ovaries.

"I'll give you a call when I get the results back," Ian said as he walked Helen back to the waiting room.

"Now for you Flippers – come and let me see if you are doing the right thing."

Mark went through the standard checking procedure that the doctor did for all his intending fathers. A blood sample was taken to be sent off at the same time as Helen's.

"There is one more thing that you are going to have to do for me. I'm going to need a sperm sample from you – you as a researcher will know what is required, so let's arrange a time. How about tomorrow?"

Mark kept his appointment with the clinic and he was told the results within minutes.

"Nothing wrong with you in that department, mate!" Ian said, and then added. "Perhaps when the tests come back we will know a bit more."

A week had passed when Ian came to the house. Mark was at home by himself – Helen was out shopping.

"Got the results back today. Appears everything is right with you, but there might be a small problem with your wife."

Mark suddenly felt uneasy. "What do you think it is Doc, not anything serious I hope?"

"Probably nothing major but just enough to stop her from

getting pregnant the usual way. I'll do a couple more tests to see if we can overcome the glitch," Ian replied.

Over the next few weeks Helen went to Ian for further checking. She had to endure more tests and more poking and prodding and the embarrassing internal that Ian politely passed over to a female colleague at the clinic to do.

On Helens last visit to the clinic the doctor had requested that Mark also attend next consultation with her.

"Well, I've got good news and a bit of not so good news for you," Ian said to them as he peered over the latest test results. "It seems that Helen can still have children. There is a slight abnormality in her fallopian tubes that appears to be the stumbling block. With some medications I can prescribe, it may take a year or two before everything is functioning as it should. If you want a quicker outcome then maybe we should be looking at IVF treatment. In the meantime, I am going to consult with a colleague of mine – perhaps find an alternative solution. For now I suggest you go home and have a good talk. If then you decide to go in the IVF direction – we can have a real good chat about it over dinner next Saturday night."

As expected the subject of conversation in the Britcher house for the following week centred on having a baby. Mark made it positive that he would stand by any decision that Helen made. It would be her decision to go ahead with the invitro program. Her needs came first he affirmed. Helen seemed to want more reassurance than that from Mark. Her maternal instincts craved to have a baby.

"Mark I do really want for us to have a baby – a child that we both will love and share," Helen said.

"Then that settles it!" Mark stated as he hugged her. "Tomorrow we get the ball rolling and with a bit of luck in a years' time, 'we', will be the proud parents of a little Flipper or Helena."

Dick and Dora were now being prepared for release and Mark was re-assimilating them to the wild. A section of the huge net was left open, allowing them to come and go as they desired. Any reliance on being solely fed by humans could end. Mark noticed that Dora was reluctant to go out of the ring and hunt with her mate. Mark decided to confine her to the catching section and re-check her health.

Something was peculiar with Dick's attitude towards Mark. He appeared to resent Mark being near Dora. During an examination and temperature recording procedure of her, Dick made repeated charges at Mark.

"What is wrong with you?" Mark yelled at Dick. Perhaps it was the new-found freedom the dolphins were experiencing after being confined for several months. Mark was a cautious man who was not about to take any further risks with heavy-weight Dick. With own his safety a concern he made a mental note to next time lock Dick on the outside of the pen before he entered the water to examine Dora.

Back at the Science Centre laboratory Mark tested and filed the last batch of blood samples he had taken from Dora. "Stupid me," he berated himself. "She's pregnant – no wonder Dick is so edgy."

For the next few days the bay was too rough to venture out to check on the dolphins. Mark stayed in his office inputting the data he had collected to his computer. A graph showed there had been a regular rise and fall in Dora's body temperature. With this information he believed he could now pinpoint the days that a dolphin could become pregnant. "Success at last," he gloated to himself. "But I need a few more pieces of data to verify my finding – I had better get some more samples and readings from Dora before I let her go."

The following day was still blustery but Mark was a man on a mission. "Bugger the weather; it's spoiling a good day," he joked to himself as he positioned his rolling research boat alongside the net pontoons. "Must lock Dickie Boy out today – don't want a repeat of the other day."

Mark closed the section of net so that Dick was kept on the outer. Dora seemed happy to stay inside and keenly accepted the morsel of food that Mark gave her as a reward. The water was choppy and a few larger waves occasionally pushed through the net wall tossing both him and Dora around in the surging sea. This made it difficult for him to do his necessary tests on her. An unexpected larger wave rolled Dora over on to her back in the examination net. Instead of being her normally sedate self, Dora reacted to the sudden shock. She began panicking, making squealing sounds. Mark tried to roll her onto her belly to calm her.

Being in a rush to get the samples, he had not put on his swim-fins and was unable to get enough power by his kicking legs to shift her weight. Dora kept on thrashing about and squealing. Throughout the time the dolphins were in the enclosure he had never seen her so distraught. The thought flashed through his mind "Perhaps being pregnant has changed her attitude."

Suddenly it felt as though his ribs had been hit by a sledge hammer. Dick had leapt over the pontoons edge wall into the pen and was ramming Mark. Another violent 'Thump', hitting Mark in the solar-plexus, knocking his breath from him. Several more attacks from Dick were sustained on Mark rendering him unconscious. His limp body sank slowly into the depths of the net.

That evening, after a visit to the clinic, Helen sat waiting for Mark to return from his work. She had important news to tell him. Now there was no need to do the full IVF program – all that was required was to implant Mark's sperm into her fallopian tube. A simple procedure that can be done at her next ovulation! Excitedly she waited.

'Eight o'clock he's not normally this late?' She nervously thought. 'I'd better call him on his mobile. The phone rang for the standard 30 seconds then clicked into the message bank. *"Hi, this is Mark – Probably underwater at the moment – leave your number and I'll return the call when I surface,"* was Marks recorded reply.

"Honey – hurry up and come home, I've got lots to tell you," Helen anxiously said after the beep.

Another ten minutes passed without Mark responding, so Helen rang the laboratory.

"Good evening – Science Centre Lab – James speaking – can I help you" He rattled off in parrot fashion.

"James is Mark with you?" Helen enquired.

"No, he's not here," James responded then continued to explain.

"I haven't seen him all day – he went out to the dolphins this morning and as far as I know he's not back yet. Hang on I'll give him a call on the radio."

James put down the phone and went into the radio-room and tried calling Mark.

"Helen I'm not getting a response on the radio so I'll have to go outside and use the night vision binoculars and see if the boat is still out there. I'll phone you back,"

James went out to the sea-ward side of the building. From here he could see almost the entire bay. With the powerful ex-navy night-vision glasses he could he could see that Pisces was still tied alongside the net pontoon. No lights were on, which was out of character for Mark. He always insisted that everyone was to use the riding lights at night when working at the sea-pen. James rang Helen back. "It looks like he's working late out at the net. I'll try him a few more times on the radio and get back to you when I know what times he is coming home."

As James walked away from the phone uneasiness overcame him. "That's not like Mark at all – he always lets Helen know if he is working late. The 'tinny' is still down at the waters-edge I think I had better take a quick trip out to the boat and check – just in case," James said to himself.

It wasn't long before the outboard powered 15 footer was skimming over the now calmer waves of the bay. As he approached the research boat he could not see any movement.

'Perhaps the bugger has climbed into the bunk and having a sleep' he joked to himself trying not to think the worst.

Once along-side Pisces, James grabbed his torch and started calling out "where are you mate? – Come-on! Wake-up! - your missus wants you to get home.'

Nothing was heard.

A horrid sick feeling raced through James when he found the cabin empty. Back on deck he could see Mark's testing equipment in handy reach of the pontoon side.

"Where are you Flippers?" James yelled as he shone the torch back and forth across the water. Dick and Dora were swimming slowly around the enclosure staying close together.

"MARK! Where in the hell are you?" James knew that onboard the boat they kept a very powerful spotlight. He dragged the long cord out onto deck and switched on the light. His first instinct was to scan the pontoon. Nothing! Then he quickly swung the light, checking the water around the boat. Nothing there either. He shifted the beam back into the pen and tried to see down into the dark water. The reflecting light bounced back at him making it hard to see anything.

A splashing sound came from the other side of the pontoon.

"You bloody idiot Mark, you scared the shit out of me, for a while I thought you were a goner," James yelled across the water as he swung the light towards the noise.

There he saw that it was Dick splashing near the net curtain. He would dive down then resurface then slap his tail on the water.

"What's he bloody doing?" James wondered, now beginning to panic.

Dora joined in the splashing and diving down with her mate. James kept the light shining in their direction. What in the hell is that? It was hard to make out at first but Dick and Dora were trying to lift something to the surface.

"Shit its Mark," James screamed as he clambered across the pontoon ring to the dolphins. In his haste he had dropped the spotlight on deck. Its powerful beam was shining skywards and only a small amount of light was illuminating the pen surface. As James neared the commotion, the body of Mark was at the surface being held there by Dick.

"Please, oh please don't be dead" James cried as he laboured with the lifeless Mark straining to drag him onto the pontoon.

In the poor light James could see that Marks face was a sickening ashen grey and he probably had been dead for at least three hours as rigor mortis was setting in. James instinctively knew that nothing could bring his mate back to life. Tears cascaded from his eyes as he pulled the stiffening body around the pontoon then onto the deck of the research boat.

"May-day, May-day, May-day this is Pisces. Come in please," James's quivering voice called on the radio.

"This is Coast Watch receiving – Please identify yourself, what is your position," crackled through the speaker.

A trembling James replied to their request. Bravely he contained his grief and used all his self-control to continue speaking and inform them of Marks drowning.

The answering operator sensed the distress in James's voice and sensitively called back *"Can you stay at the sight mate? We will get the police out to you on the SES Emergency Vessel straight away. They won't be long and can you turn on the deck lights."*

James hung the microphone back on its clip. The deck lights were now on and the radio was silent. An eeriness permeated the boat.

James went out on deck and sat with the lifeless Mark. The adrenalin from the event was beginning to subside causing him to shake uncontrollably.

More tears flowed involuntary as he sobbed. "What bloody happened? How am I going to tell Helen? She relied on you – she always has. What am I going to say to her?"

As James sat with Mark it seemed as time had stood still –

His thoughts wandered back to their college years when he and Mark studied together. He remembered being best man at their wedding and how much Helen and Mark were in love.

"How could this happen to you – you never did anything wrong. You never harmed anyone. What happened?"

The sound of the motor of the approaching SES boat snapped James back to reality. He wiped the tears from his eyes as he reached out and took the rope from the deckhand clad in orange overalls, then tied their boat alongside.

"Are you OK," a policeman said as he climbed aboard.

"I think I'll be right," James replied.

"Can you tell me exactly what happened" asked the Officer as he looked at the lifeless Mark

James related to him everything that had transpired. While he told his story the Officer took notes and called on his radio for an ambulance to meet the boat at the Stenross boat ramp.

"Come on let's get your mate back to Lincoln. Are you able to handle this boat or do you want one of the SES lads to deliver her home for you" he asked as he put his arm around James's shoulder.

"I would like to be with Mark a bit longer if I could – he was my best mate and I won't be seeing much more of him again – it would mean a lot if Mark and I can do this last trip together," James requested as the tears again filled his eyes."

"Not normal procedure but I do understand" the officer replied. "We will follow behind you just in case it gets too much"

"Thanks! I would really appreciate that," James's quivering voice replied.

The ambulance crew met both vessels at the boat ramp. Marks body was taken away in an ambulance. James went with the police to the station to finalise and sign his statement.

Ever since finding Marks body, one thought was dominating James's mind. 'How am I going to break the news to Helen?'

At the police station it was arranged that a woman officer would drive James back to the Science Centre for him to get his car. Then together they would go to Helen to break the sad news. The female officer would be there as support for Helen when James was to tell her what had happened to Mark.

As the police-cars headlights shone down the driveway of the Science Centre they could see Helen standing next to the building.

"She must have walked here looking for Mark – How am I going to tell her?" James nervously questioned the officer as Helen rushed towards the patrol vehicle.

"Try to keep calm if you can," replied the constable quietly as James was hastily undoing his seatbelt. Helen flung open his door before his fumbling hands had managed to unclip the unfamiliar buckle.

"James, what's happened – where is Mark?" Helen blurted out as James climbed out of the vehicle. All he could do was to hug Helen and repeatedly say "He – he – he's – he's..."

Helen pushed away from James's hold. Her face had gone white.

"Where's Mark? – Where is my Mark? - Tell me James what has happened!" she demanded.

Huge tears were flowing from James. 'He's had a fatal accident Helen, I'm so sorry. He's dead, and we don't really know how it happened."

Helen started shaking, her arms then reached out for James "NO, NO he can't be – tell me James, please tell me he's not," she wailed. "No he can't be, not now, not now" She blubbered, tears poured from her eyes as she fell into his arms.

James held Helen tightly.

Several times she thumped his chest with her closed fist then screamed. "He can't be – not Mark – he can't be – not now – we haven't had our baby yet!"

For many unbroken minutes James held Helen as they cried together. Their emotional release was so great; the police woman who had stood in background also had tears trickling down her face.

Gradually Helen's bawling subsided to sobbing. James's eyes were red from his crying – his shirt saturated with Helens tears. In a quiet voice the officer offered to drive them back to Helens house.

"No, no thank you; I want James to tell me everything now" Helens shaking voice replied as she led James to the rocks that lined the foreshore of the Science Centre. Glancing back to the officer as they walked away James said "I have my car here. We'll be right, thank you."

The moon was rising over Boston Island its light shimmered on the now calm waters of the bay, little waves splashed gently on the sea-front rocks near where Helen sat with James as he imparted the events of that evening. Helen sat in silence, interjected only with a deep gasping sob as she listened while James tried to speculate what may have happened to Mark.

"Something must have gone terribly wrong somewhere, somehow. He knew his job so well. He was the best diver around here," James offered as a comforter to Helen.

"When will we know, how are they going to find out?" She quizzed him and slowly regaining a modicum of her composure.

"When I was at the police station they said the coroner will investigate and let us know what happened – might take a while," James said as he stood up and suggested to Helen to move from where they sat.

"Come on I'll take you home."

"No thanks, I want to be alone for a while – I'll walk from here," she replied.

"Are you sure? What say I ring Kerrie and Julie for you – I'll get them to meet you at your place," he said as he pulled his mobile phone from his pocket. "Yes please – They need to be told what has happened. I wouldn't know how to tell them," She apprehensively said as more tears again filled her eyes and rolled down her face.

As Helen walked the short trail along the coastline to the house, memories of Mark flooded her mind. Many times Mark and she had walked this way together. It wasn't until she saw the *Amethyst* anchored in the moonlight at Shelley Beach that she now felt horribly alone. Helen shuddered at the thought of being abandoned. No Mark, no child. Thoughts of 'What will I do without him', raced through her brain.

All the lights were on at her place. Kerrie being first there had let herself into the unlocked house and was busy making coffee. The very pregnant Julie arrived just as Helen opened the side gate of the property. Spontaneously they rushed together into each others arms.

More tears and lots more crying as her emotions spilled over to her best friends, until all three became a blubbering confusion. Slowly they regained their self-control. Eyes gradually dried as they sat together drinking the hot coffees

Kerrie had made. Having such good friends gave Helen the feeling that she was not going to be totally alone. This was reassuring for her. It was now well past two o'clock and Julie suggested that getting some sleep would be a good idea.

"We can stay here with you" the ever-caring Kerrie offered.

"Please, do stay," Helen said as she walked towards the bedroom. "You can use the spare rooms, the beds are already made."

For the next week Helen moped around the house. Julie and Kerrie did their best to comfort her through her grief. Ian popped in several times to check that Helen was coping with the stress and caring for her health. The thoughtful James came each day and brought lunches for everyone with him. Helen knew she was surrounded with true friends but they would never compensate for Mark and for the baby they would never have.

Marks funeral came and went. Several hundred relatives and friends attended the grave-side service at the North Shields Cemetery.

The Coroner made is findings known. His conclusion was that Mark appeared to have been crushed between the boat and the outside of the pontoon ring, but he could not explain how Marks body was found inside the net.

With many questions left unanswered Helen began to isolate herself from the others despite their efforts of support. Her once fit body had become thinner and her tanned skin had faded to pale cream. Ian recognised the signs of depression and prescribed the appropriate medications. Kerrie balked at that idea of using chemicals and offered her natural remedies on several occasions. Because Ian's treatment was basically working Helen politely refused what Kerrie was recommending. However, Kerrie could see that her best friend was not handling the strain of the situation, even with the doctor's medication.

After another week of sitting watching Helen become more vegetative and disconnected from her friends. The ever-caring Kerrie brought Helen a book on 'overcoming losses.'

"Thanks for your kind thought but a book won't bring Mark back, will it?" Helen said as she took the book.

"No it won't – but it might help you get through your heartbreak," Kerrie replied.

Helen put the book on her dining table and said politely, "Thanks, I'll have a look at it later."

Two days passed and the book remained untouched on the table. Helen sat down to write thankyou cards for those that sent their condolences. As she was pondering what to say in the cards the book caught her attention. Picking it up she flipped through its pages briefly reading a line or two here and there.

One passage stood out as if speaking directly to her. *'Each person's journey through life is theirs alone – parts of which may be shared with others – along this path we encounter many happenings – all events are for a reason – only time will reveal what this purpose would be.'*

"What bloody reason would there ever be for my love to be taken from me,": Helen yelled at the book as she threw back onto the table.

Just as the book hit the table the phone rang. "She's having her baby," Kerrie's excited voice declared over the phone. "Come around quickly Helen – Julie is in the birthing pool and her contractions are really close now!"

Instantly Helens grief was pushed aside. Her friend was having a baby and she wanted to be there. It took only a few minutes to get to Kerrie's clinic. Helen arrived as Kerrie was instructing Julie to 'push, push it is nearly there, just a few more pushes, you can do it.' Within moments Julie groaned a gigantic aaaarrrgghhh!

"It's out – It's out – it's a girl, you have a girl," Kerrie excitedly announced as she lifted the baby from the water into Julies arms.

At that very moment every depressed thought and self-pity mindset was lifted from Helen. Her tortured mind had suddenly snapped back to reality. No longer did she blame the world for cheating her of her husband.

She now had a purpose – she too was going to have a baby. Even though Mark was dead she knew exactly how it was going to happen.

"Ian, I want to have a baby," Helen announced to her Doctor at his clinic. "I've stopped the medication you had given me because I am no longer feeling depressed."

"Helen that's dangerous," Ian replied "stopping anti-depressants suddenly can have side effects – you should have asked me first," then added. "Are you sure you are well again? - I had better give you a good checking over right now before we discuss this baby thing." Ian completed all the checks needed and realised that indeed Helen was once again herself.

"What is all this about a baby," he said as he unplugged the stethoscope from his ears. "Well, you know what I need to do to have a baby – so let's do it," Helen said whimsically to Ian.

"Who do you have in mind as the father?" Ian enquired in a serious tone. "Mark," replied Helen.

"Mark? You mean your Mark!! You can't bring back the dead, come on, be sensible Helen," the perplexed doctor exclaimed.

"I have a plan," Helen said excitedly "James told me that before Mark died he froze straws of his semen and it is in the liquid nitrogen flask at the research centre – he did it that time you were testing his sperm count."

Ian continued to consult with Helen. "I must warn you that there is a high probability of Mark's sperm not being viable. It may not deliver the result that you are expecting', he stated with doctor-like authority.

Unperturbed Helen persisted, "Ian, I must try it is my only chance. Let's try it anyway'.

Reluctantly Ian agreed but added the proviso that if it were anyone else but her, he would not get involved in such a madcap plan.

"You are going to need help from the Fertility Clinic on this, and by the way you are talking you want to get started as soon as possible Eh? – I'll make the arrangements – but first I'll need the frozen sperm – so it can be tested."

Immediately after her consultation, Helen went directly to the Science Centre to tell James her news. "I always thought you were crazy, but now I'm sure you are," James said after listening to what Helen had planned with Ian.

"Let us not get too excited until Ian sends the stuff away to get tested" James said as he opened the liquid nitrogen filled flask. "There are four straws frozen in here, three with naming labels and one with just a letter M," James said as he inspected the writing on the labels. "Britcher Zero One, Britcher Zero Two and Britcher Zero Three, that's what is on those labels – we had better not give Ian that other one to send away – could be any-ones or any-things." James said as he replaced the lid on the flask. "Leave it with me Helen. I'll organise the transfer of the three straws to the clinic for Ian – I will have to get another liquid ice container to ship them away. They can't have this one, there is some tuna DNA tracings in it as well that I need to keep frozen."

The frozen straws of sperm were sent to be tested. News came back to Helen via Ian that all three straws were viable and Helen could undergo the fertilization program using them. Arrangements were made and Helen did regular trips to the Adelaide clinic.

Five months passed and she had not yet become pregnant. So far the treatment was not working. "Not many more chances left," the Adelaide Doctor informed her. "We have almost run out of you husband sperm," he added.

This was not the news Helen wanted to hear. In her mind she knew there was still hope that one day she would be carrying Mark's baby.

The day finally came when the last drop of sperm was inserted into Helens eggs. "Let's keep our fingers crossed with this one," the Doctor said to Helen. "Your Doctor Ian, will let me know how you get on. Best thing for you to do now is relax and let nature take its course,"

Back at home Helen was unable to do what the Doctor had suggested. She knew this was her last chance at pregnancy. Every second day she self tested with the home kit – each test the same – not pregnant. Three weeks elapsed before a reluctant Helen had the heart to visit Ian to have a confirmation test done by him. The results were confirmed, this round of implant had also failed. Ian did his best to console Helen.

"Perhaps one day you may meet someone else and by then you could possibly have a child with him," Ian said to give Helen some hope.

"No Ian, it will never be the same for me again – I loved Mark so much – it is his baby I want – no one else's," she said in a soft subdued voice as she walked head-down towards his office door.

For the entire next two weeks Helen languished around the house until she realised that no one had been to check *Amethyst*. Helen rowed the little crib dinghy out to the boat. Mechanically she did the necessary regular checks of the vessel and ran the bilge pump to clear any water that may have entered the hull. Everything was as it should be. Satisfied that her check was complete Helen sat for a while on the lounge in the cabin. Her mind occupied with thoughts of Mark. It was on this boat that she first saw how handsome Mark was, she mused, as she lay back on the soft leather lounge.

All of a sudden she sat upright. 'There is still another straw of semen at the lab – you silly bugger Helen!' she loudly chastised herself. Without hesitation she leapt out of the cabin and locked it. Jumped into the dinghy, almost tipping it over, then hurriedly rowed back to shore where she dragged the craft above the high water line, then jogged along the trail to the Science Centre on her now urgent mission.

"James! James!" she yelled as she approached to him as he sat on the Centre verandah. "Is that other straw of frozen sperm still in the flask," she asked.

"Yes it is still in the container, why do you ask," he replied then paused "We don't know what is in it or where it came from."

Helen then posed the questions, "Is there any way that we can check what is in the straw. Can we find out if it is more of Mark's?"

James said, as he looked directly into Helen's eyes. "If you thinking of doing more IVF, you have to remember that Mark was meticulous with everything he did. He must have had a reason for not labelling that particular straw. It could be anyone's or anything's."

"Can we find out what's in it," Helen pleaded.

"I suppose I could remove a small portion and test if it is sperm. Big problem is sperm from higher order mammals looks very similar. Hard to tell exactly where it came from unless I send some away for further analysis."

"James I have to know, will you help me find out. Please do what is necessary, it's the only chance I have," Helen begged as she pressed her hands in the praying position.

Reluctantly James did as his friend requested. First he checked the frozen product was actually human sperm. Being unable to accurately ascertain that the sample was from Mark or some other source, another portion from the straw was forwarded to a specialist laboratory for a more comprehensive study.

Unfortunately the specimen sent by James was ruined during transport and deemed useless for testing. A failure in the container sealing ring allowed the material inside the cask to become thawed. Another portion was requested.

Each new test required one quarter of the straw to be sent away to be analysed.

James's initial test and the spoilage had already accounted for half. Now another twenty five percent was going to be risked. This effectively left only the one last quarter still available for Helens treatment.

Ten days passed before the testing laboratory made email contact with James.

Their letter stated; 'Rather unusual specimen. As far as we can ascertain it is human. We did a cross reference with the data at the IVF clinic. Most of the sample matches that of her late husband. However there is some unidentifiable contaminants present in the specimen submitted for testing. In conclusion we would advise any portion of the sample not be used for IVF purposes and all remaining product be destroyed.'

Helens hopes crumbled when James showed her the email. For several minutes she remained silent a she paced up and down his office then turned him and asked, "Please don't destroy what is left in that straw. Not until I have time to think about everything. Once that is gone – so is Mark – forever. My dream of having his baby is finished too."

"Using anything from what is left would be a waste of time and money. Perhaps your dream was not meant to be. Maybe it is time to let go and stop frustrating yourself." James said with sincerity, paused then looked at Helen "Holding frozen samples is an expensive exercise for the Centre and that straw has to be removed. Best I can do is keep for another two weeks. Then the space will be taken by POMS disease specimens from the oyster industry. Sorry, that's the best I can do."

A dejected Helen slowly walked home to her empty house. No Mark nor baby to greet her. 'There is still hope until the straw is destroyed. There must be a way. Can't give up now, I have to keep trying, but how?' she repeated to herself as she sat on the lounge chair looking out over the bay. Weakening to the strain of the emotionally hectic day she fell asleep in the chair. A crazy mix of dreams raced through her head until one particular reverie startled her and she awoke suddenly. Stunned by the vision of watching a young boy swimming under the water alongside the *Amethyst*, Helen's heart pounded. It took several deep breaths to regain her composure as she contemplated the meaning of what she had dreamed.

"Hi Jules," Helen said with excitement as she phoned her friend. "Hey what do you know about dreams?"

"Why – did you have a special one?" responded Julie. "Only high impact dreams that you are able to remember after waking up have any relevance. Most of the others are just your brains way of dumping accumulated trash thoughts. Bit like the delete button on your computer."

"This one certainly had an effect on me. I dreamt I was watching my boy swimming underwater when I was on the boat. Freaked me out." Helen confided.

Julie then rambled on about other people's dreams and how she interpreted each one and the outcomes of her often requested predictions.

"Yours might be an omen or a conclusion to something. What is your heart telling you?" Julie asked in a matter-of-fact way.

"Silly question. You know I want Mark's baby."

"The one thing I tell everyone is; Dreams will not come true unless you actually do something to help it to happen. Do nothing and the dream will simply fade away. That's the best advice I can give you."

"Oh Jules, you really are a beautiful friend. Thank you so much. Love you, bye." Helen said as she a she finished the call.

The two week deadline urged Helen to hatch a risky plan which would then need to be put it into immediate action.

Letting Kerrie know was the first crucial step. Helen rang her number only to hear a recorded message.

After the beep Helen hastily barked into her phone "Hi Kez, Please call me as soon as you get a free moment. Need to discuss something urgently. Luv ya." then rushed over to her computer and began typing 'Fertilization using donated sperm' into the search bar.

Helen poured over dozens of the written articles to learn more about the different processes used to inseminate in order to achieve a successful pregnancy. One article caught her attention.

IUI, the full title being Intrauterine Insemination. Over and over again Helen read the technicalities of this procedure. "This is what I should have done in the beginning," she told herself.

"Yoo-hoo! Are you there Helen," came Kerrie's voice from the front door. "Got your message – it sounded like you needed me in a hurry. Had a gap in my appointments, so here I am. Is there anything wrong?"

"Oh no Kerrie, nothing wrong, for a change something may be right. I have a great idea of how I might get pregnant but I will need your help to do it." Helen could barely contain her excitement as she moved away from her computer desk, then gave her friend a bigger than usual hug.

"What is this fantastic idea you said that you needed to tell me in such a rush?" an inquisitive Kerrie queried.

"Promise you won't laugh or say I am stupid" Helen said then began to relate how she thought the idea of IUI using the remainder of the sperm in the straw might work for her.

"Mmmm, It's a crazy idea that has possibilities," Kerrie said as she held her chin while looking out the window. Then slowly added "What if James won't let you have the straw. What will you do then?"

"I wasn't going to tell him because he wants the stuff destroyed. I thought I might sneak it away when he was not looking," Helen said flippantly.

With a doctor-like attitude Kerrie probed her friend. "That must be the maddest plan I ever heard anyone concoct. You intend to steal the straw out of the flask. How will you keep it frozen until you can use it? Getting it is one thing, but using it definitely has its risk and there is no guarantee it will work."

Helen went quiet and sat back at the desk and opened the page on the computer where the method she proposed to use was outlined. "Kez please read this and tell me if I am barmy. Doing this is the absolute last chance I will get to have Mark's baby." She moved aside for Kerrie to sit next to her.

Kerrie read the article through twice then commented. "I can see why you think it might work, but percentage wise, you would have a less than ten percent chance. Most of the problem will be having an ovulation begin within the next ten days. Not to mention the fact that you do not have the straw in your possession."

"Never thought about that." Helen replied. "Since Mark...' she paused then gulped before finishing with, "I have been having regular periods. They should be due next week, I think."

Kerrie looked at her wristwatch, and walked towards the door, "Have to go, my next appointment is due in five minutes. I must be as crazy too. I won't have anything to do with the 'acquiring' part. Probably get a prison sentence if I got caught. However I will help with the insertion. That part of the procedure has to be done by a professional. Must use sterile instruments or unwanted infections might mess up everything. Luv ya, you crazy lady." Then with a goodbye wave she exited the house.

After listening to what Kerrie had said, Helen remained seated at the computer contemplating how she might dovetail all things necessary to at least try her radical idea. Making time to visit James was her priority and decide to phone him.

"Science Centre, Good afternoon this is William Scott, may I help you?" crackled over her phone.

"William, this Helen Britcher, is James in today?"

"Sorry Helen, James is away for the week. He will be back in his office next Tuesday," Will replied.

Then as quick as a flash Helen asked, "Is his lab open? I left a book there I had borrowed from the library that must be returned in a few days."

"Did you want me to find it for you?" Will enquired without hesitation.

"No need to take you away from whatever you were doing. I will pop down tomorrow and look for it, thanks for offering," Helen said before hanging up.

Helens brain was working overtime. She needed a distraction at the Lab to give herself time to grab the frozen straw from the holding cryocask. The bigger problem was how to keep it frozen at a low enough temperature.

Then she remembered Julie performing one of her mystical dances using something very cold to give the effect of a mist floating low to the ground.

Another quick call was crucial.

"Hi Jules, I have a question for you. Where did you get that frozen stuff you used when you did your dance in the mist?"

Helen asked.

"Did you like it – it was my re-creation of Kate Bush dancing to her song Wuthering Heights. Magic wasn't it."

"Yes I did, it was lovely. Only someone like you could perform that dance to make it look so fascinating," replied Helen, then asked the important question "Julie, how and where did you get whatever it was?"

"That was just some stuff I got from Roger, the Vet. Why do you want some? I think he likes me and will probably let me have some more. He also has the special container to keep it in. It looks just like a thermos for keeping tea or coffee hot, but it has liquid nitrogen in it. Mustn't ever put your finger in it or you will get frostbite," Julie replied in her unmistakable dipsey voice.

"Can you get some tomorrow morning and the container too?" Helen asked.

"Why do you want it – are you going to dance?" her friend giggled.

Helen then revealed her plan to Kerrie.

"Will we be wearing Balaklava's?" chuckled Julie.

"No we won't. We will just act normally when we go into the Science Centre. Let's hope they will not suspect what we are doing. Your job will be to keep William amused while I nick the straw." Then she realised no book of hers was left behind so it would be necessary to smuggle one in, using Julie's large hessian shoulder bag. In the bag would also be the flask.

"See you tomorrow afternoon and don't forget the container and your big shoulder bag. Bye and thanks." She put down the phone.

Next morning Helen awoke early, too anxious to sleep.

Through the night she had meticulously gone over her modus operandi of obtaining the straw from the laboratory.

Nervously Helen waited for her accomplice. In her mind she rehearsed the plan of action for grabbing the straw whilst Julie distracted William.

It was a relief when Julie called in her sing-song voice "Helen – where are you?" from the verandah then popped her head in the doorway.

"What are you doing wearing that mask?" the now uptight Helen growled at her friend.

"Robbers wear masks and we are going to rob the place, aren't we?" Jules giggled like a young schoolgirl, as she removed the disguise, then as she put a friendly arm around Helen said, "No need to get serious, it's going to be fun. If James thinks we are up to something he could spoil our chances. So I have decided to be my usual self and not act like a robber. That way he won't suspect anything. You had better relax too or he will get suspicious."

"Relax, you say relax, getting that straw means everything to me." Helen abruptly stated as she walked into the kitchen area. "I need something to settle my nerves. Let's have a cuppa before we go. What would you like, tea or coffee?" as she plugged in the electric jug.

"Just a glass of water for me," replied Helen. "I am off the hot drinks, Kerrie keeps telling me I need to drink more water."

"Speaking of Kerrie, I had better tell her that this afternoon we will be getting the stuff. She will have to look after it until …" Helen paused for a full minute when it sudden became apparent what the next step the venture would involve.

"What say we phone William to see when he will be there?" Julie suggested to snap Helen out of her wandering thoughts.

"Hi William, Helen Britcher here again. Just wondering if you will be around the Science Centre this afternoon?"

"Should be back in after my lunch, probably about one thirty. If it is that book you are after, I can help you look for it. I will inform the front desk you are coming, that way you can come straight through to my office." Offered a very obliging William.

"Thanks Will, but it shouldn't take me long to find it. See you then, bye."

As the two would-be thieves drove down the Centres driveway, Helen again went through their plan. "You keep Willy amused and I will get the stuff. I will have the bag on my shoulder ready with the flask. You did bring the flask?"

"Stop panicking, you are beginning to make me nervous. Of course I bought the flask," Julie said gruffly.

"Just act normal," Helen whispered as they entered the main door.

"I have come to collect a book from William," she informed the young lass at reception.

"Good afternoon Mrs. Britcher, Firstly, may I pass on my condolences? I had worked with Mark and he was always talking about you and how you were trying to have a baby. He would have been a wonderful father."

Her words momentarily floored Helen almost making her forget the purpose of their mission.

Helen replied, "Yes, Mark would have been a great dad and having a baby was our plan, but sometimes things do not go the way you want."

"William is expecting you. Not sure if he is back from his lunch break. Would you like me to go and check?" the receptionist then asked politely.

"No need, we can wait in his office if he is not there. Which one is his," replied Helen.

"It is the sixth door on the left down the corridor, his name is on the door. I will show you which one, just in case," the girl replied just as her phone rang.

Taking advantage of the distraction caused by the incoming call, Helen gave a polite wave gesture and the two amateur crooks set off down the long corridor.

Four doors down Julie nudged Helen. "Look this one is marked laboratory."

"No, that's the student lab he sometimes shared with James. Will's office is further down the hall. The vial was always kept in the research Lab. It's the next one along."

She took the next few paces to Mark's old work area. "Try the door to see if it is locked," She whispered as they stood nervously looking back and forth along the corridor.

Julie's hand grasped the door knob, then slowly turned it. The door was unlocked. Carefully she opened it just enough to see if anyone was inside.

"It's empty," she said with a big smile on her face.

"I'll go in – you go down to Wills office and keep him busy," Helen said in a whisper as she once again looked back toward the reception area.

Being again in her husband's laboratory almost totally un-nerved Helen but she was on a mission to save his genes. Her heart was racing as she took several deep breaths to settle her nerves while looking around the room to locate the cryoflask.

'There it is' she muttered to herself as her eyes locked on to her target. Then she remembered Julie's warning and that Mark always wore insulated gloves whenever he open the flask.

Another quick look around the room was needed. "Where are they," she moaned just moments before she sighted the pair on a lower shelf.

The next step was to open the cylinder and find the right straw. With the screw cap off, Helen could just see the contents held in the icy vapour. Several straws were marked with code numbers. Three had the words BF Tuna another two marked Albacore. One appeared devoid of any markings. Helen rubbed it with her glove to check.

"That must be it, only has the letter M written on it, just as James had told me," then sighed in relief as she took the borrowed flask from her bag unscrewing its lid.

Carefully she withdrew the length of glass tubing from its icy storage and slipped it gently into the flask then sealing the lid.

Hurriedly she place the container into her bag. "The book, the book. Mustn't forget the book," she uttered to herself as she grabbed the book out of the bag then placing it on a close-by shelf.

Getting the lid back on the large cryoflask was harder than expected. Ice had formed around the top rim which needed to be removed before the lid could be refitted. Thankfully the gloves were protecting her hands from the extreme cold as she hastily rubbed the ice from the cask threads.

Finally the lid was positioned to reseal the contents in their frozen state.

Unexpectedly the laboratory door opened. Helen was terrified, dreading that she had been sprung so close to getting her hands on the frozen sperm. On Impulse she flung the gloves off, both landing under the bench alongside her.

"Just me – did you get it?" Julie whispered to her startled accomplice as her head peeked around the now open door.

"Shit Jules!! You scared the hell out of me. Where's William?"

"He hasn't come back from lunch yet. I waited for a while outside his office. Thought he may have come here. Well Cat Woman, did you get it?"

Before Helen could answer, William's face also appeared in the doorway.

"Sorry I was late, got held up chatting with a colleague in the carpark. Have you found the book you were after?" he said as he entered the room and walked towards where the two stunned women were now standing.

Helen could see that her book was sitting on a shelf almost in view William.

Quickly she turned her body to face him in order to obscure the book and partially hide her accomplice. Sneakily Julie slipped the book off the shelf then discreetly passed it to Helen behind her back.

"Found it," Helen exclaimed as she held the book above her head then quickly placing it into the bag, she had automatically slipped over her shoulder.

"Looks like you didn't need me after all," William said completely oblivious of what had occurred a few moments earlier. The three casually exited the lab then he courteously walked with them towards the Centre's entrance foyer.

"Must have a look at your art one day Julie. James told me how wonderful your work is." William said still totally unaware of Helens real mission in the lab.

"Thanks for the compliment," Julie replied as she gave William an appreciative peck on the cheek to disguise her guilt of being a partner to a misdeed.

Helen's hands were about to push open the exit door when the receptionist announced in a demanding voice "Mrs.

Britcher wait one moment please."

'Oh no! I have been caught' raced through Helen's mind. Immediately her pulse rate climbed rapidly to a point where she could feel her chest thumping beneath her blouse.

"Y-yes, anything wrong," she nervously replied.

"You haven't signed in or out. It's a new rule, all visitors must sign the book when visiting." She insisted as she rotated the book on the counter and held out a pen for Helen.

As the two robbers drove up the steep driveway of the Centre, Helen shakily said, "Phew! That was too close for comfort. I thought the receptionist was going to ask me to open the bag. If William had arrived ten seconds earlier than he did, I would have been caught red-handed or should I say glove-handed," then gave a huge sigh of relief.

A few minutes later. "Kerrie, Kerrie I have got it. What shall I do with it," an excited Helen squealed into her phone.

"How long was it out of the nitrogen, did it defrost at all," Julie clinically replied.

"Nope, just took it from the big flask and put it straight into the small one. I have it in the car with me now?" Helen said eagerly.

"That's good, bring it to my clinic, I will look after the container until you are ready. Speaking of ready, I need to monitor your ovulation temperature. We will do that at the same you deliver the straw." The doctor in Kerrie requested.

Kerrie had only to monitor Helen for the next few days. Her examination on the third day confirmed that the timing was right for attempting Helen's only remaining hope of having

Mark's child.

That morning, in her own meticulous way Kerrie prepared both the pilfered specimen and Helen ready for implanting.

Although the process was a clinical procedure, it was also a quick and simple exercise for both patient and practitioner.

The short time it took Kerrie to complete the necessary steps amazed Helen.

"Gee that was much quicker than the times I underwent IVF. Are you sure that's all we have to do?" She quizzically enquired.

"That is my bit done. The rest is up to what happens inside you. However you can help by not swimming, taking hot baths or doing anything that requires strenuous exertion for the next few days. Go straight home and lay down for the next hour, preferably on your stomach. No alcohol, smokes, pills or potions. Just let nature do its work. I will do a simple blood test every day, just to keep an eye on things." Kerrie quoted doctor-like to her patient then gave her a big hug of caring friendship then added, "Apart from that my dear, cross your fingers and hope for the best. And not a word to anyone about who was the donor or where it came from. Promise."

As required, Helen reported daily to see Kerrie. On each occasion Julie would be alongside her anxiously waiting for some good news. On the sixth visit Kerrie informed Julie "Your chances of becoming pregnant are decreasing rapidly. Normally at this stage I would recommend the procedure be done again. However, in your case that would be impossible as that was the only remaining sample available."

Tears of despair flooded Helen's eyes. "There must still be a chance. How long before we know for sure?" She pleaded.

"Normally the maximum life of the sperm would be six or

seven days. We have already reached that." Kerrie said gently. Then Julie wrapped her arms around Helen then looked her in the eyes "Sometimes we have to accept that our dreams may not have been meant to happen. We feel your pain and ..." then tapered off talking as the two shared the sadness of the moment.

That night unable to sleep Helen lay in her bed softly talking to her Mark. "I tried. I really tried. I wanted to have your baby. My dream was so real. I believed it was meant to be. I love you so much and this was my last chance. Oh, Mark if you can hear me, please make my dream come true," then sobbed tears of anguish flowing down her face until she fell into a deep sleep of emotional exhaustion.

The first hour of her sleep comprised of jumbled dreams that were a mix-mash of doctors, test tubes, blood samples and calendars. Intertwined with these were office girls, babies, friends and birthing baths, her mind apparently dumping an over-load of the many recent stresses and unanswered questions. Finally her body's need for uninterrupted sleep shut down the clatter in her head and the muddled apparitions evaporated allowing her to sleep soundly for the next few hours.

As the hour before dawn approached, the sleeping Helen entered into a surreal encounter with Mark. Gently he kissed her neck as they lay in bed. She could feel his body against hers. Tenderly he held her in his arms and whispered softly "Don't despair my beautiful Helen, our son will soon be yours." Then, like a lifting mist he was gone.

"Flippers, Please don't leave me," Helen cried out as the

undeniable reality of the vision startled her out of her sleep.

For a while longer she lay, continuing to feel his presence in the room, then she looked towards the ceiling and said softly "My wonderful husband, you did hear my plea. I love you so much."

A new-found confidence enveloped Helen, replacing a fear of failure as she arose from her bed. Something extraordinary had stemmed from her dream encounter with Mark.

Her prior doubt of not getting pregnant had been overpowered by a more positive confidence.

While waiting for her morning oatmeal to cook, Helen reminisced the evening when they were told that Julie was going to have a baby. Then her thoughts drifted as she remember saying to Mark that she also wanted to have a baby and how he surprisingly agreed by saying "let's start tonight." Then she remembered Kerrie bringing a pregnancy test kit a few weeks after that.

"A test kit, got to get a test kit today," she spoke out aloud as the piping hot porridge was poured into a bowl.

The chemist did not open for business until 8.30 giving Helen enough time to sit quietly and enjoy her breakfast while musing on her earlier dream of Mark's foretelling visitation.

The purchase made, an eager Helen returned home, threw her car keys on the table and headed hastily towards her bathroom.

"Yes, yes. I knew it," she squealed reading the positive result on tester. "Mark, Mark, you beautiful man, I am pregnant – we are going to have a baby,"

Kerrie was perplexed by the result of Helen's self-testing. Why hadn't the blood tests detected the onset of pregnancy?

Being qualified only as a natural birthing practitioner Kerrie recommended Helen make appointments with Doctor Ian to undergo ultra-sound examinations over the coming months as he had the appropriate equipment for doing such tests.

It was not until three and a half months later that any outward sign of being in the family way became obvious. A baby bump was beginning to form and was quite noticeable when Helen went for her once-again regular morning swim.

Snide comments, "Wonder who the father is. Has she got a new man?" were heard from two old biddies who also took a morning dip in the same location.

Their gossiping intrigue never phased Helen in the least, for she knew that there was only one man in her life and he was certainly the father.

On her first visit with Doctor Ian, he unwittingly placed Helen in a tight spot when the question was posed. "Well Helen, who is the lucky man?"

Her doctor's involvement with the IVF attempts meant that serious questions would be raised as to how the sperm was obtained. This necessitated Helen becoming allusive.

"Sorry Ian, at this point of time I would prefer not to divulge who the father is. All I want to do is have a healthy and happy baby. After it is born I will let everyone know."

"On the birth certificate we are obliged to include the father's name, if known? So in the meantime it is your little secret, eh!" Ian said in a voice of authority. Then he paused and looked directly into her eyes, the spoke in a slightly more serious tone, "Mark and I had been friends for a long time. We often shared our deepest thoughts and from what he said, I thought you and he were inseparable. I never expected you to be so swift in replacing him. You certainly have kept your new romance a well-kept secret. I hope it does not involve anyone with commitments to another family?"

"Ian, to put your minds at ease I have not had it off with someone with 'commitments'. Mark always said that he could trust you. It is not that I do not hold the same trust, but having this baby is all I care about. So please do not think badly of me. All I want is for the baby to be born, then I will tell you everything. Please give me that time." Helen pleaded.

Over the coming months Helen's, now growing larger baby bump, had tongues wagging. Malicious rumours abounded that she had been having affairs with multiple men and could not directly pinpoint who was the father. Apart from her friends, Kerrie and Julie, no one else knew the secret of her pregnancy. Ian attempted on each of her consultations to solve his curiosity, asking Helen if she was ready yet to allow him to know the fathers identity. Each questioning was answered with Helen's polite answer. "After it is born."

Exactly two hundred and eighty days after the implantation Helen began to feel powerful contractions that signaled the time had arrived to give birth to her precious child.

"Kerrie, I am having contractions, should I come now?" an eager Helen said over the phone.

"Relax Helen, seeing this is your first baby the early contractions will always feel quite strong. You probably have a couple of hours yet. Let me know when the contractions are getting closer together," Kerrie calmly replied, then suggested that Helen get Julie to drive her to the clinic – just in case.

An astute calendar watching Kerrie had already prepared the large birthing-pool two days earlier and brought the water slowly up to constant body temperature.

Within an hour of Helen's initial call to Kerrie, Julie walked the beginning to stress, very pregnant Helen into the birthing room. "Looks like you are further advanced than I had previously thought. Better get you into the pool," a now concerned Kerrie suggested.

The warm glow of candles flickering around the room combined with soft background music created an environment of tranquility that gently calmed Helen as she disrobed then entered the pool whilst being reassured by both her friends.

"Relax and lower your body slowly into the water. Lay on your back, stretch out your arms and float. Take long slow breaths to maintain your calmness and let each contraction flow gently from your womb to your hips. Your baby will stay calm if you do too," Kerrie soothed her as she positioned Helen's head on the cushioned edging of the pool.

Helen lay floating for only a minute then she cried out a terrifying "Arrrgh" as an extremely powerful contraction pulsed through her body and caused her to tightly squeeze Julie's hand she was holding.

"Relax, take a deep breath in, then slowly out, relax and let it all happen, don't fight the pain. It is your baby wanting to come into the world," Kerrie assured her without adding any anxiety to her patient.

"You can stop squeezing my hand now," Julie said jokingly moments before Helen let out another slightly more subdued "Ahhh! Oh Mark! Ahhh!" as further spasms of pain ran through her pelvis, she again applied more pressure on Julie's hand.

"I can see the top of the head," Julie screamed forgetting all about her crushed hand.

"Now, big deep breath and push on the next contraction,"

Kerrie said clinically as the midwife in her, slipped into her well-practiced birthing routine.

Then as she was about to say 'You are nearly there' Helen's baby slid painlessly out into the water.

"It's a boy, it's a boy," Julie squealed excitedly then repeated "Helen, it's a boy, Mark would be so proud if he were here."

"He is here, I can feel him," Helen said with tears of joy flowing freely from her eyes.

"Did you see that?" Kerrie asked as she went to lift the baby into Helens arms. "He kicked both his feet at the same time, not once but twice. It looked to me as if he wanted to swim," she chuckled.

The huge smile on Helens face told its own story as she held her newborn against her body.

"Don't need to ask you to smile for the camera," Julie said as she took a photograph with her smartphone, before adding "Got a name picked out?"

Helen looked down at her baby, "Yes we have. Mark and I said if we ever have a boy, his name will be Fynn Markku. It is a tribute to where Mark's dads was born – Finland, plus it has a marine theme about it. Markku was his grandfather's name. Not hard to guess who Mark was named after. Probably only use Fynn, it will be easier to say and spell."

It took several months for the town gossipers to find another subject for their wagging tongues to talk about. At first Helen would become emotionally hurt whenever she overheard her name being mentioned in any supposedly 'not meant to be heard' close by nudges and whispers regarding her baby. Gradually she was able to shrug off the innuendos about her moral character. One look by her at the baby was enough to affirm that Mark was definitely the father.

Helen's life now revolved around 'their' son. Fynn was growing into a healthy, strong infant. It was unmistakable that the boy had no fear of water. From the very first wash, whenever bath time came around he would become excited and relish every moment of being bathed in Helen's small plastic baby tub. It was difficult for his mother to hold him as his little legs would kick and splash continuously from the moment he entered the warm water. Often he would wriggle enough to slip from her grasp and become completely submerged. When Helen regained her grip and lifted his head from below the surface a positive look of glee radiated from Fynn's face and the kicking and splashing would continue with even more vigor.

"How could you not like the bath, with a father such as Mark and his love of the sea, and my swimming – it was inevitable that you too would be at home in the water," Helen said lovingly as she lifted little Fynn from the tub and wrapped him snugly in a soft towel.

For the first few weeks Kerrie had overseen the baby's health needs. As Fynn neared the one month old stage she suggested to Helen that it was time to include Ian into the boy's life. Immunisations, health checks and circumcision would need to be addressed and could no longer be avoided. Helen would have to face him and reveal what she had done to have the pregnancy.

"You worry me. What if there was some exotic bacteria in the stuff you stole? You actually broke the law to get something, but you had no idea what it really contained and then you coerced a couple of anonymous friends to assisted you become pregnant with the stolen article. Helen, you did everything you should not have. But luckily for you nothing went wrong." Ian berated her after she now revealed to him, how baby Fynn had been conceived without divulging her accomplices.

Indignantly he stated, "If you were not Marks' wife, I would have suggested you consult with another doctor or maybe a psychologist as well, rather than me. Your late husband was such a good friend of mine. However, I owe it to him to take care of both you and your son. From now on you will do everything by the book and I mean everything!" Ian stated in his most officious overtone. "Now let's have a good look at the lad and make sure that everything is as it should be," he growled.

Ian meticulously gave baby Fynn a host of checks, took blood a sample, a DNA swab and a stool sample extracted from a timely soiled nappy. "Make an appointment to see me again in ten days for the results and hopefully you will do nothing silly in the meantime," Ian said somewhat still obviously miffed, as he lifted the baby from the examination table then handed him back to her then began noting everything on his computer.

Once outside the clinic and at her car, "Whew! That was an ordeal. I have never seen Ian so angry," Helen said to Fynn as she placed him into the baby safety capsule. "Hope he has calmed down by next week."

In the back of Helen's mind had always been a miniscule thought as to the sperm that she thought to be Mark's. Was actually his. There was a reluctance within her to see Ian again, for fear that he had proven Mark was not Fynn's father, a thought too terrible to contemplate. Helen knew the issue had to be resolved to remove any iota of doubt, so that she could one day look her son in the eye and say with positivity that his

Dad was definitely Mark.

Doctor Ian appeared somewhat calmer as he ushered Helen and the baby into his consulting room. "First of all Helen, I am sorry that I had been short with you last week, please accept my apology. Your actions were reckless and it took me a few days to realise how desperate you were to conceive Mark's child. Now I understand why you did what you did" as he looked over the results on his computer screen.

"Good news is," then he paused, "Congratulations! The tests reveal that Mark is definitely the boy's father, however there is a slight inconsistency with the DNA strand that we are unable to explain. Seems that young Fynn has an extra gene in the chain and I am puzzled as to what it represents. I did a check on both yours and Marks and the additional gene does not show in either." Ian said, then continued with the remainder of his report. "The other tests came back to indicate your son being hale and hearty except for one anomaly that was found in the blood sample. For some reason his oxygen capacity level in the blood was equal to that of an athlete in training rather than an infant. Just to make sure the test was not inaccurate I will have to send a second sample off for analysis."

Weeks went by and young Fynn began to crawl. Often Helen would take him to the beach and let him feel the sand and touch the water with his feet as she dangled him at the water's edge. With every little wave that splashed his legs, baby Fynn would squeal with delight.

On one occasion after having placed him on a towel to dry his legs, Helen was momentarily distracted by a flock of seagulls squabbling over a fish carcass thrown to them by a fisherman cleaning his catch on the nearby rocks. In those brief seconds little Fynn had crawled the two metres to the water then into shallows.

"Fynn!" Helen frantically yelled as she observed her baby heading for deeper water. As each incoming wave smacked into the little tykes face he would giggle and keep going forward. Helen rushed in and snatched her son out of the water. Her baby's displeasure was obvious when he began to cry while at the same time trying to wriggle from her grasp. Noting his reaction, Helen then lowered him back down into the sea. Immediately the protestations ceased and he splashed his hands and feet in much the same action as doing the doggy paddle. "You like that. You certainly are Mark's son," she said, then lifted him out again only to be greeted by another session of bawling. Helen then squatted and held her squirming son again into the water. "Looks like I will have to keep an alert eye on you. You have no fear of getting wet. I reckon it is time for swimming lessons to ensure you are safe," she said to him as he kicked his feet in sheer delight showering her with the splashes.

Helen was an excellent swimmer and could have taken the time to teach her son how to swim. However she had heard there were several aspects regarding a child's confidence in the water that she thought better to be left to the qualified experts that undertook teaching the young ones.

Helen went to sign up young Fynn for the toddler water safety introduction at the Leisure Centre pool, but due to the large number of young participants, she was told the group her son was to attend, was not beginning until next month. 'Just have to watch him more closely' was made as mental note in her mind as she handed over the course fees.

It had been two weeks since Julie had been to visit Helen and her baby. "Want to go for a beach picnic next weekend with some friends," an excited Julie announced as she bounced into Helen's house prior to giving her friend a lingering hug. Before Helen could reply, Julie blurted "Peter and I – we are going to get married! Our beautiful daughter Saffron, will now have married parents."

"That fantastic, I am so glad you two are finally getting hitched," Helen said excitedly, then added "When is the wedding?"

"Next Saturday – on the beach," Julie giggled. "Pete wants it to be a casual affair with everyone dressed in beachwear – you know kaftans and bright shirts. Lots of colour. It has to be a fun day for everyone."

Helen happily replied "I wouldn't miss this one, it sounds like it is going to be another of your crazy ideas that will actually work. Yes, Fynn and I will be coming."

Colour was certainly the theme. Everyone was outfitted in an array of brightly coloured clothes. Even the usually straight dressed doctor, Ian, jazzed himself up for the occasion, wearing lavender shorts and pastel multi-flowered Hawaiian shirt topped off with a white broad-brimmed sun hat tied around with a primrose ribbon.

James excelled himself with an outfit of brightly coloured batik printed pantaloons, no shirt over his tanned skin and his chest bedecked with hippy beads.

Helen chose a colourful traditional Fijian Sulu (skirt) offset with a bright red bikini top discreetly hidden behind several rows of floral leis. She had dressed Fynn in a blue and white sailor suit. Kerrie rose to the moment with her brightest pink flowing beach skirt and wide sleeved loose blouse under a huge floppy beach hat. Even the conservative William, from the Science Centre, had managed to find a pair of brightly coloured shorts and a tie-dyed tee shirt to wear.

Julie and Pete looked as if they had both stepped out of the pages of a sixties hippy party. Barefooted Pete dressed in pale blue harem pants and balloon sleeved shirt, ornamented with a large round peace sign charm, and hung on what appeared to be old rope. Jules clad herself in flowing white muslin material decorated with a dozen brightly coloured scarves tied around her waist. Her long hair, bedecked with a single bright orange hibiscus and a spray of frangipani flowers pinned one side of her head, emphasised her 'child of the earth' natural beauty. Young Saffron was wearing a miniature version of her mother's outfit except for the tiny violets pinned in her hair.

After the exchange of vows and the presentation of rings and signing of the register the newlyweds invited those present to enjoy the sun, beach and refreshments and stay for a party to celebrate their marriage. Those savvy to beach weddings had prudently included their swimwear under their colourful clothes and took a refreshing plunge before joining the party mood.

Helen sat young Fynn, now eight months old, on a towel under one of the many beach umbrellas and gave him a floral garlands to amuse himself, then went over to the shade shelter where drinks were being served. It was a festive occasion. Helen opted for a glass of bubbly for herself and a small glass of juice for Fynn. Drinks in hand she headed back to the spot that she had left her son. Momentarily a dreaded thought flashed across her mind. She had left Fynn unattended and him being attracted to the water. Drinks in hand, her pace quickened to a jog towards the umbrella. She expelled a sigh of relief when

Fynn was sighted happily pulling each flower from the garland. "Having fun," she said with a relieved smile to him as she offered him a sip of the cool drink.

A Marimba band snaked cheerfully into the wedding area playing catchy calypso music. Julie and now husband Peter, each with open bottles of champagne, danced arm in arm to the music among the guests refilling their glasses. "Come on Helen get in the party mood – have another Champers," Jules quipped as she topped up Helen's now empty glass. For Helen it had been a long time since there had been an occasion to let her hair down but having Fynn with her, bought with it the need for responsible parenting. With this in mind Helen deliberately sipped only slowly from her glass of the tantalizing wine, as she watched the others begin to revel in the swing of the celebration.

The party-lifting music had an effect on even the most staid of guests. The usually reserved William was dancing to the beat. "Wanna dance," he asked Helen as he sashayed barefooted towards her with his half full wineglass in one hand and a bottle in the other. "Thanks for asking, but no thanks," Helen replied. "Well if you are gonna just sit there I had betta refill your glass," he joked as he poured what was left in his bottle into her glass then sat on the sand beside her.

"You know what," he slurred then continued, "I did an inventory the other day and it seems there is one straw missing from the lab freeze container. You wouldn't happen to know anything about that would ya?"

Helen had for a long time pushed aside any thought of being found out for stealing the straw. It never occurred to her that all the items in the laboratory were logged and recorded. She should have remembered that Mark was a stickler for keeping records. "Don't know anything about it – What was in it?" Helen replied guardedly.

"Don't know – just listed as M in the ledger," William said as he drained the last dribble of champers from the bottle into his glass. "Mark never entered its contents into the log, just the letter M."

"What about that dance," Helen gushed out to change the subject.

"You're on," came William's instant response as he grabbed Helen's hand then began doing his interpretation of a Caribbean dance. With the champagne bubbles already starting to take effect on Helen she spontaneously mimicked his cavorting and let the rhythm of the music flow through her body.

"Looks like you two are having a good time," Julie said as she passed her bottle of bubbly to William then added a cheeky grin and a wink of preempting his intentions with the single parent Helen. Then out of the blue added, "Where's Fynn?"

"He's sitting under the umbrella," the dancing, now light-headed Helen replied.

"Can't see him," Julie said in a matter of fact tone.

Helen stopped her cavorting then instantly dropped her wine glass and shrieked without thinking about her language. "Shit! he's not there," then looked towards the water.

Had she been a second later she would not have seen his entire body disappear under the waves. Immediately Helen ran out towards the spot where her son was last seen. Without hesitation, she dived into the water. Her fears were justified when she saw the submerged body of Fynn. In panic Helen hoisted his seemingly lifeless body to the surface then rushed him back towards the shore.

As her feet touched dry sand young Fynn's eyes opened then began to giggle and lifted a shell he was holding towards his mother face.

"Oh God – you are alright. Can't take my eyes off you for moment! You scared the heck out of all of us you little bugger." Helen said as she wrapped her errant son in a towel then gave him a hug of sheer relief, while Fynn held out his arm to proudly display his shell to those, mouths still agape who had watched the drama.

"Looks like you have got yourself a diver," the partially inebriated William said as he began to pour drink into the glass that Helen had hastily discarded.

"The water is like a magnet, looks like I will need to tie rope to him. That way I can just drag him out," Helen said agitatedly as she grabbed the glass from William and took a large swig of the champagne to calm her nerves.

Fynn was now over a year old, walking, and baby talking. *Amethyst* had laid idle on the mooring during Helen's pregnancy and the birth of her son. Luckily the hull was sound and had been well coated with anti-foul. Despite that, marine weed growth was accumulating under the waterline. Knowing this Helen organised the local boat slip to have the yacht brought up in a cradle for maintenance and a clean. It was arranged that Fynn would stay ashore with Kerrie rather than have him aboard while the difficult procedure of cradling the boat was in progress. On the morning of slipping, Kerrie rang Helen to tell her she had an urgent dental appointment and was unable to care for Fynn. Because Julie had already let it be known that she was flying to Adelaide the previous night Kerrie decided to take a chance and take Fynn onboard for the short trip to the slipway.

Having had that earlier scare with Fynn and now being totally safety conscious, Helen set an example and put life jackets on herself and young Fynn before placing him in the dinghy. Fynn's face was beaming with smiles of delight as Helen rowed toward *Amethyst*.

"You are a bit like your dad – he loved being on the water," Helen joking said as they pulled alongside the yacht. In her heart she was so glad to see that some of Mark's nature was in the boy. As Helen lifted Fynn aboard the yacht, his instant reaction of pure pleasure confirmed that their son was also born with a love of boats and the sea.

While *Amethyst* motored towards the boat-yard Fynn's eye were glued on the pair of Dolphin that scooted in out of the bow wave. Excitedly he pointed to them and giggled with approval of their antics.

The task of centring the yacht's keel in the cradle, for some was difficult, but with Helen's years of experience onboard the family's boats, *Amethyst* was position exactly and then cradle and boat were winched up the rails and out of the water. Helen passed young Fynn down to a worker who had secured the lines to hold the vessel upright while on 'the hard'.

"Oh my god" Helen said as she clambered down the ladder. "If Mark were here to see this he would have a fit. There is more weed on her than in my garden!"

Don't worry missus – won't take long to water blast all that off – but gotta get to it before it dries out." The worker then grabbed the high pressure hose and began directing the powerful water stream towards the hull.

With a clean hull and a fresh coat of anti-fouling, sailing *Amethyst* was again Helen's choice of weekend fun. Even though young Fynn had attended water safety classes at the Leisure Centre, to ensure that he was secure, Helen rigged a clip-line and put a harness on him whenever they were afloat. This allowed the youngster free movement onboard but he could go no further than the stanchions on the deck perimeter.

The best boating weather in that beautiful part of the world is in autumn. Easterly breezes and low swells made for pleasurable days on the water. Fynn had now started school. On some weekends Helen and Fynn would camp overnight aboard *Amethyst* in the shelter of Memory Cove or the calmness of nearby Spalding Cove. Young Fynn was in his element. In the relative safety of Spalding Cove mother and son would swim before partaking of a seafood breakfast. Eagerly Fynn would tuck into the freshly caught and cooked fish. Having a son with such a happy disposition, coupled with his acceptance of being onboard the yacht reminded her of the many days Mark and her spent exploring the coastline and islands that abounded Spencer Gulf. Mother and son were happy, but often her tears would dampen the pillow as her thoughts drifted back to the days when Mark was her sailing companion and shared the bunk and cuddled her until they fell asleep.

By the time Fynn was eight, he could take over the helm and steer *Amethyst* in a straight line. On occasions when Helen went below to make a cup of tea or prepare a sandwich she would catch a glimpse of his beaming smile as he sailed the boat by himself. What thoughts were going through his head she wondered? Was he just glad to be out sailing or was he dreaming of being Skipper of his own boat. There was no doubting now that Mark was Fynn's father despite some earlier reservations as to the origin of the frozen sperm.

With Fynn attending school and her having some part-time work in the Fisheries Department office, Helens life was now rediscovering the routine she had prior to Mark's death. Laboratory assistant William had been promoted to senior researcher for the Marine Centre and trainee Rodney had filled William's vacant position. Marks best friend James' role was now senior marine biologist. He was now concentrating on the dolphin research program in place of Mark.

William had always an eye for Helen yet kept a polite distance whenever the group of friends would meet for coffee. His discreet but obvious liking for her had not gone un-noticed by Helen and she was flattered to think that as a single parent, she could still be deemed attractive. However her love was for Mark and the welfare of their son was paramount in her present life, thus, kept her feelings guarded and chose to keep William only as a close friend with no encouragement to enter a relationship with him.

The winter "blew its guts out," – one of the worst seen for many years, according to the local fishermen and sailors. *Amethyst* was now securely moored in the Marina. Helen and Fynn were basically confined to the house for those three months, apart from checking the boat and running the motor to ensure it still operates. Then as the spring weather took control, their yearning to be back on the water was foremost in their thoughts. Coinciding with first week in September was William's birthday and it had been suggested by Julie during a 'catch-up' phone call that a harbour cruise aboard *Amethyst* would be a great venue for them all to get together and celebrate the good weather and William's special day of turning forty.

"That is wonderful idea" Helen said prior to "who is going to make the food?"

Julie paused then answered –"what say we all chip in. You make one of your yummy Pavlova's, Kerrie do the salads, 'cos that her style of food, and I will do the chicken and cold meats – how does that sound eh!"

"That means the blokes do nothing," Helen said indignantly before adding, "What say we get Doc Ian, our wine buff to choose the wine and Roger and William to bring the beer, cheese and nibbles and James to organise a birthday cake and some icecream for the children?"

"Perfect," replied Julie "Leave it to me, I will get Pete to let everyone know what job they have to do."

The party mood was evident as each guest boarded the yacht. Earlier that afternoon William had already imbibed a drink or two with a few of his friends and was 'ticking over' before they had motored out the channel into the bay. Being a good skipper, Helen asked each guest to put on her recent purchase of the latest self-inflating thin profile life jackets. With a bit of strap adjustment and a heap of giggles each person – children included (Julie and Peters daughter Saffron and Fynn) were now wearing a life vest.

As the sun set behind Winter Hill the lights of the town began to reflect on the shoreline. The bay was calm with only a slight off-shore breeze. Helen simply put the idling engine in neutral and allowed the yacht to drift while the platters of food were placed on a table in the centre of the deck. Wine and beer glasses were steadily refilled. Non-alcohol drinking Helen asked Fynn to keep watch for any other boats that might come close as they partied and chatted.

Soon after the platters were emptied of their wares, James came from below carrying the cake he had purchased. Instead of having it adorned with forty candles there were only four large household ones each with flames dancing in the gentle breeze.

"Come one Willy – blow them out and make a wish," James announced as he held the cake at shoulder level for an unsteady William to do the deed.

"On the count of three," James said to the birthday boy. "One, Two, and –" Then just as William inhaled a deep breath to blow his candles, the yacht gave a sudden lurch and roll, sending him backwards over the rail into the blackness of the water. With no warning the forceful bow waves were unnoticed by the normally watchful Fynn who was distracted for that moment. These waves are usually caused by a distant passing tuna vessel or ship. The quite large waves travel silently across the surface until they splash harmlessly upon the shore or slam into and destabilise any boat they happen to pass.

Without hesitation young Fynn dived over to assist the startled victim. Instinctively Helen grabbed the wheel and engaged reverse gear to bring *Amethyst* back to where Fynn was holding the somewhat confused William. The pair were treading water, kept afloat by their auto inflate vests as Helen maneuvered the boat close enough for James and Ian to drag the spluttering William back on board while Fynn casually climbed the stern ladder. Helen grabbed a towel and wrapped it around the sodden Will. The grateful and now almost sober nocturnal swimmer reached out and gave her lingering hug. For a moment Helen froze. It had been many years since she was held by a man. To diffuse the awkwardness of the situation

Helen giggled and joked "You won't forget this birthday in a hurry," before giving him a quick peck on the cheek then releasing herself from his arms.

William then turned to young Fynn with an outstretched hand. As he shook the boys hand he said "Thanks mate – I thought I was a goner. If you weren't there I certainly would have panicked and probably drowned. Thanks, you saved the day."

The topic of the group's conversation at their next coffee session was humorously centred on William's lack of diving ability and the low score he collected for the execution of his reverse backflip dive. Gradually the chatter focused on how well Fynn could swim and his courage to leap into the ink-black water to assist poor William. Helen had taken for granted Fynn's swimming capabilities as they had swum and snorkeled many times when *Amethyst* was anchored in a bay. Doctor Ian added his professional opinion on how fit and healthy Fynn was looking. "Good looking young fella you have Helen. It will be hard to keep the girls away when he gets a bit older."

Helen never allowed herself any thoughts of another man in her life. The episode with William's hug triggered a reaction within her. After Mark's death, her mind was focused on the well-being of Fynn and the bonding of mother and son. Now a new dimension of reality was in need of evaluation. Helens thoughts drifted to considering that her son needed a male role model in his life. The thought of being with someone other than Mark, the man she so much adored sent a shiver down her spine, yet within her was the nagging need to be cuddled and held in a loving embrace. Helen's mind struggled with her love of Mark and what might be construed as a betrayal of that love and the rising necessity to once again have a man in her life.

Instead of hiding behind the fear of the truth, being able to talk candidly was something that Helen had vowed to do with Fynn. As the various subjects arose that needed to be discussed, when the time was right, Helen would openly chat with her son to keep his mind free of the bogey's that might haunt his thinking in later life.

However, the death of Mark and the birth of their son had not fully been disclosed. The subject of how he was conceived had never been discussed as she was waiting for the appropriate time and the maturity of Fynn to understand it all.

The pressing need to broach the subject of William had arrived. "Fynn, we ought to go and check *Amethyst*," she said to her son after they had just finished their lunch.

When on board Helen directed Fynn to check the aft bilge while she did a quick clean of the forward cabin.

A few minutes later, "She's dry as a bone," he announced as he stepped down into the stateroom as his mother emerged from the forward cabin and headed for the dining settee and beckoned him to sit with her.

"What do you think of William?" she openly asked.

"He's OK but a gets a bit tiddly when he has had a few drinks, apart from that I like him," came his reply.

"The reason that I am asking is that I would like a man-friend. I know Willy is keen on me, but I will not take it any further unless he is someone that you feel comfortable with. We have always been a two person family and because your father died before you were born you have never had a man that could be a role model to you."

"I get your drift," answered Fynn. "But Mum… you have taught me everything I need to know about boats and the sea. What can William add to that?

"Not much about those things, however I am sure he has a lot of knowledge about other things. He has a degree in marine biology – like your dad – plus he is a great mathematician and writes beautiful poetry. However if you are not at ease with him around I shall understand." Helen said as she looked knowingly her son.

"Don't get me wrong – William is a nice person, what worries me is why he has never married," Fynn said softly and smiled.

Several weeks passed with no further mention of William.

Lower Eyre Peninsula's weather was now in summer mode. *Amethyst* was once again the weekend home for the sailing Britcher's. Helen had confidence with her now 12 year old son's ability to manage the vessel should anything unforeseen happen, the outlying islands of the Sir Joseph Banks Group was a selected destination. With the breeze tending from the south-west, barefooted Fynn took the helm and sailed the yacht the 30 kilometre run to the Group, keeping to the east of Spilsby Island whilst Helen sat on deck soaking up the warm sun rays. Haystack Bay on Reevesby Island provided a sheltered anchorage for an overnight stay. Sharing the bay was an outboard powered half-cabin runabout. The two men aboard gave a friendly wave as *Amethyst* dropped anchor at a respectable distance away from them. Before the yacht had settled back on her anchor rope Fynn had a line in the water to catch some squid for tea. Within minutes the lad had two nice sized ink-squirting cephalopods in the plastic fish-bin. "You caught them; you clean them," Helen reminded him as she went below and began to peel some potatoes to make fried chips for their evening meal. Fynn actually enjoyed cleaning and gutting the fish he landed. He saw it as being part of his little bit of stewardship of the sea. The family motto was – 'only catch enough for you needs and leave some for others'. As Fynn was rinsing the long white bodies of the catch he happened to glance towards the other vessel. One of the men was standing on the stern quarter-deck waving, trying to get their attention.

"Mum! Mum! I think those blokes need us – one is waving his arms about. Reckon I should slip the inflatable in the water and go over to see what they want. You stay here and crumb the squid."

With a quick pull on the two horsepower outboard starter cord of the little craft he headed over to the other boat.

"What's the problem?" young Fynn asked as he pulled alongside.

"Bloody anchor rope is wrapped around the prop and the running tide is keeping tight so we can't lift the motor to untangle it," the fatter of the two blokes said.

Fynn maneuvered his rubber boat towards the stern. His first reaction was to ask himself, "How did they manage to get a forward line around an aft outboard leg?"

The rope had jammed itself in the propeller blades and the taut anchor section was holding the motor hard against the hull.

"No hope of getting that loose until the tide stops," Fynn said with boyish authority then added as he tethered his craft to theirs, "My motor is not strong enough to tow your boat against the current. Only other way is for me to dive down and pull the rope to loosen it enough for you to raise the leg." Before the men could ask any questions, Fynn stripped off his shirt, dived over the side and disappeared under the hull. Nearly a minute passed then he emerged and yelled more instructions "Soon as you see it go slack – hit the leg-lift button," then the lad vanished again. Both men peered anxiously at the small part of the tight rope that could be seen. Another three minutes passed before suddenly it went slack and the leg was raised. Next moment Fynn had his feet against the boats transom whilst pulling with both hands on the anchor line. "I'll hold this part while you flick your loose end over the prop," he barked his orders. With a bit of rope fumbling by the two on board, the propeller was soon free of the entanglement.

"Thank heavens you showed up – we would have really been in trouble if we couldn't get back to Tumby!" said the thinner bloke as he realised that their saviour was still just a young boy.

Without pausing to seek any praise for his effort Fynn gave the men a wave and headed back to *Amethyst*.

"What did they want?" enquired Helen as he pulled alongside the yacht. Fynn replied jovially "The idiots had their anchor-line wrapped around the prop. Had to dive in to untangle it."

"You be careful in the water around here," she said with concern. "A big White Pointer haunts this area, so keep your eyes open – better still, keep out of the water at dusk and dawn. Sharks often feed at sun up and sun down."

"Mum, it was still daylight," he replied.

The episode with the anchor rope and the aroma of frying chips had increased Fynn's hunger for tea.

"Oi! Put that back and wait," she lovingly chastised him as he grabbed several pieces of the salad that was cut up and ready to serve with the evening meal. "Too late," Fynn giggled as he stuffed a piece of tomato in his mouth.

The chips fried and the crumbed calamari cooked to perfection, mother and son sat on deck eating their food. The sea was calm and the warm late afternoon air created a perfect ending to the day. Noting the red glow on the west horizon Helen said "It's going to be a nice day tomorrow too, red sky at night – fisherman's delight."

"Is that just a saying or is it true?" Fynn enquired.

"Most of the time," his mother replied. Your father explained to me that the red glow is caused by the sun, now far in the west, is not shining through any clouds. No clouds means a clear next day."

"What was Dad really like?" he asked as he reached out and held his mother's hand.

Helen put down her almost empty plate and put her arm around him. "Your Dad," she paused for several moments, "You are just like your Dad. You remind me so much of him. The way you stand, the way you handle a boat, your love of the water and how your care for the environment – in fact nearly everything you do, is as if Mark is here. Your father was my soul mate, my best friend and most all, he gave me you. I will always love him."

Fynn dropped his head as a tear rolled down his cheek. "I wish he was here, I wish he hadn't died, I wish I had a Dad." He gulped as more tears began to flow.

"I do too, I do too," she said softly as she gave him a lingering hug after which mother and son sat in contemplative silence and watched the sunlight disappear from behind the island.

The next morning they were awakened by the two blokes in the other boat shouting "Ahoy!! Are you up yet? – got some fish for you."

Helen slipped on her shorts and top then emerge out of the cabin. The boat had pulled alongside. One of the men was holding onto *Amethysts* gunwhale while the other was taking some large whiting from his insulated fish box then placing then in a plastic shopping bag.

"Just wanted to say thanks for getting us free of the anchor rope – here's some nice big whiting we caught last night," the fat one said as he passed the fish to Helen.

"That lad of yours," – then tilted his head and looked Helen in the eye – "That lad of yours," then paused momentarily "What I am trying to say is that lad is something special – He knows what he is doing and never hesitated to help us. We have never seen anyone that could hold their breath as long as he can – must have huge lungs. Anyway, thank him for us, will ya." Then the other chap released his grip allowing the boats to gradually part before motoring slowly away.

"Will do and thanks for the fish," Helen called out and waved as they left.

After a sumptuous lunch of some of the freshly caught whiting and salad, the breeze, the now freshening north-easterly was touching 10 knots making their exposed anchorage a little uncomfortable. "Let's take advantage of the wind and head for home," Helen suggested. With no need of any further encouragement the young sailor began prepping the yacht for the run home. "Slow down there laddie, no need to rush," mother said as she cleared some loose gear from the deck.

Fynn was a man on a mission. His eagerness to get sailing

was obvious. Like a seasoned professional he started the motor and slipped *Amethyst* into forward gear in order to retrieve the anchor. With the anchor safely up and lashed to its holding block Fynn unfurled the jib then began to set the main while Helen took the helm and headed the boat out from the bay until enough air filled the sails so the motor could be cut.

"Move aside bosun – let the Skipper take the wheel," Fynn cheekily announced to his mother as he nudged her away from the helm. Helen went below to tidy-up the galley table. Looking up through the hatch she watched Fynn keeping the yacht on course. His young face radiated a huge smile. Like his father he was in his element, on the water, sailing a boat. Her eyes filled with tears she reminisced on the days when Mark and she spent weekends sailing off to some secluded bay. "I miss you Flippers," she said quietly as she glanced towards an old photograph of him that had been pinned above the chart table.

After several more weekend sailing trips, summer came and went. The coolness of autumn altered Helen's priorities. The weekends aboard *Amethyst* now showed her garden had been neglected and was in dire need of some TLC.

Fynn helped by doing the mowing and trimming back the overgrown bushes. The cuttings were piled in a heap. "Looks like you will have to borrow the Doc's trailer to cart that lot away," he said to his mother as he pointed towards the large pile of offcuts.

Helen phoned Ian and was told that William had borrowed his trailer last weekend and was due to return it soon. Ian suggested Helen phone Willy and ask him to drop it at her place instead of his. Within an hour an eager William was reversing the trailer into the Britcher's Power Terrace driveway.

"That was quick," Helen chortled and walked towards him as he began to uncouple the trailer.

"When you finish – instead of taking it back to Ian – can you bring it to my house – still got a bit more stuff to shift," William stated as he stood up from behind his car.

"Only need it for the one load. You can have it back this afternoon," Helen replied.

"Well, in that case I should hook it back up again and help you load" he said as he waited for her response.

"That would be nice – Fynn can help too." Helen said, then without thinking put her hand on William's shoulder in a gesture of thanks.

Her unexpected touch halted William in his tracks. He turned towards her then blurted out "For you, anything – just ask," then his face reddened with embarrassment from his over impulsive reaction.

Helen looked at him and said, "You are a good man William. Thank you."

To hide his obvious blushing, William turned to look out towards the foreshore of Shelly Beach.

"Struth!!" he suddenly shouted.

"What's the problem?" Helen queried.

"Look out there," he said hurriedly pointing towards a young child drifting out from the shore on a pink plastic blow-up swan being pushed along by a brisk southerly breeze.

The obviously heavily pregnant mother was yelling frantically from the shore for someone to save her child.

Without hesitation Fynn, who was at that moment walking towards the trailer, bounded out of the driveway, dashed through the scrub that grows between the road and the shore, then scrambled down the rocky cliff that surrounds the Shelly

Beach cove.

Hopping on one leg at a time he wrenched off each shoe as he rushed towards the water, dived in and began swimming with powerful overarm strokes towards the errant swan. Even though his swim speed was faster than the rate of drift, the now screaming terrified child had floated another fifty to sixty metres further out into the bay.

"Look at him go – never knew that he could swim so fast," William puffed as he and Helen ran towards the panicking mother.

In less than a minute Fynn had reached to child and began to tow the swan by one wing to the shore. "Hang on tight and I will get you back," he reassured the now crying lass.

With the swan and child nearing safety the mother hurriedly waded out up to her waist and snatched her offspring from the plastic pool toy and began to scold the child for wanting to bring the swan to the beach, leaving Fynn holding the swan.

"I told you not to bring it – didn't I? See what happens when you don't listen," she blurted at the shivering and sobbing young girl.

Rather than be caught in the heat of the moment, Fynn walked across the sand, tied the dangerous toy to the tree that shades a small section of Shelley.

His mother and William had also removed themselves from the vicinity of the obviously very irate parent and were now standing on the access pathway steps.

"Job well done," said William as Fynn leveled with them on the step. "Pity the child's mother didn't bother to thank you," he added.

Helen then said softly "I think she was so frightened of her daughter drowning that her focus was solely on that and nothing else – it is probably better we leave to let her calm down and stop chastising her child."

Then Helen added as she patted her sons back. "Fynn, just lately you seem to be always saving someone,"

William humorously piped in with, "I'll drink to that!!," as the trio walked up the steep path towards home.

Over the ensuing next few months, William's presence was seen more often than usual.

One day Fynn said candidly to his mother just after William had driven away. "He's a not a bad sort of bloke – you and him – you know what I mean."

"No I don't know – What is it you are trying to say?" Helen quizzed.

"You said once before that you would like to have a man in your life – I am sure my Dad wouldn't mind if one day you found someone to be a father to me!" Fynn said seriously as he looked her directly in the eyes.

Fynn's statement nearly floored Helen. Helen then remembered the time when she had said needing to have a man in her life. Until that moment she had always thought that Fynn's life would be nourished enough by having only a very caring mother. She hadn't realised that her son yearned for a father figure to be included in their lives.

"I am sorry – I thought," then stopped in mid-sentence and went over and put her arms around her boy and hugged him. "I didn't realise that you too wanted a man in our lives. I was so much in love with your father, I was too scared to give my love to someone else." Her eyes filled with tears.

"Dad has been dead for over fourteen years and now." He paused, then his voice trembled as he started to cry. Through his tears he blubbered, "I need a living Dad not just one from your memories, I don't have and never had a real father. When I was little, I wished that one day, I would have a dad to kick a footy with me or just hold my hand. I want that wish to come true."

"Oh Fynn – my precious son. Please forgive me. I thought I was doing the right thing. I now understand that I had replaced Mark with you. Now I can see that you also needed someone,"

He wiped the tears onto his sleeve. "Mum; everything that you have given me has been perfect. I could never have hoped for a better mother. It just…It's just that I feel good inside when William is in the house with us."

Helen regained her hug on Fynn. "I love you so much and I am sure your father would be so proud of your honestly. He would understand everything you are saying," as she lovingly kissed his forehead.

"Love you too Mum," he sobbed as they held each other in a prolonged hug.

Now that he had openly spoken about his thoughts regarding William, Fynn suggested that just the two 'men' should spend time together in order to get to know each a little more.

"Mum, what say I take William fishing on the boat. Been told some decent size whiting are being caught down Taylor's Island and Memory Cove. William has his boat license. So will you trust me with *Amethyst* without you being onboard for the weekend?"

"Am I not invited?" she responded

To which Fynn replied. "Not really – 'cos every time we go anywhere, it has always been just you and me. Wouldn't you like to have spent a weekend without me hanging around? That way you might have found out more on what makes William tick. Anyway, it was my idea – so I get the time with him first."

With hands on her hips Helen laughingly answered "For a young lad you certainly know to drive a convincing case. Perhaps you might consider becoming a lawyer?"

"No way – wouldn't do that – I want to be on the sea, not in a stuffy office or a musty old courtroom dealing with criminals," came his immediate reply.

Next weekend Helen watched from the pontoon as her son and William motored out of the Marina. A motherly flash-of-doubt danced momentarily in her mind. Then as she watched Fynn confidently handled the craft that niggling fragment of reservation disappeared completely.

Fynn was once again in his element. He had set the main sail and *Amethyst*, with a gentle sou'wester up her stern was, sailing towards Fanny Point.

"I can see that you love yachting. The speed that you had that sail locked into position shows your mother has taught you well," said William as he stood alongside Fynn observing a pod of dolphins play in *Amethysts* bow wave.

Over the previous few weeks, Fynn's youthful mind was constantly questioning if his mother and William would ever become a couple and what would be his reaction to having a 'father'. Today was the first time that the two 'men' were doing something together, like father and son. One might assume that his concentration was on sailing, but the emotions and thoughts that were bouncing around in Fynn's head were in stark contrast to his quiet exterior as he confidently skippered the vessel.

Impulsively, Fynn turned toward Will and blurted out, "Do

you love my Mum?"

The suddenness of such a question caught William off-guard. "You also can throw a pretty hefty verbal punch, I hope that was not something your mother taught you?" William went quiet.

Three silent minutes passed before Fynn again enquired, "Well do you or don't you?"

William stood staring towards the bow where the now vanished dolphin were previously frolicking. He slowly nodded his head up and down as if he were answering the question in his mind, then took a deep breath.

"I think I have always loved your mother, from the day I first saw her. However, she married your father so that was that. The fact is – I still do and probably always will. Not sure if she would ever love me? That is why I am still single. Never found anybody that could be her equal,"

"Really," replied Fynn

"Yes – really," then Will smiled and asked Fynn, "Has she ever said anything to you about me?"

"A while ago she said that you were pretty brainy and could write poetry. Not much else except you do not handle alcohol very well."

"Ahhh! – I thought there may have been something said about my getting a bit tipsy on occasions. Probably it's because whenever I am near her, I become a pack of nerves and usually end up drinking more than I should. It has always been hard for me to know what to say when she is around. I'm scared of being rejected" then he hesitated for a moment. "Many of the poems I write are about her – but don't ever let her know – promise!" He said then added "I hope you will not repeat anything I have told you – I have never discussed my feelings for her with anyone else."

"Your secret is safe with me – what is said out here, stays out here," Fynn solemnly answered as he rounded Cape Donington and headed towards Carcase Rock.

As the sail refilled and the boat settled after the turn, Will picked up the conversation. "Thanks mate – even though you are still young, I believe that you can understand my situation. The last thing I want to do is to frighten her away. I have waited many years for her. A few more won't hurt."

With a few cranks on the winch by Fynn to tighten the mainsail, *Amethyst*, helped along with that offshore breeze was making about 9 knots gliding smoothly past September Beach.

"Here – have a turn at the wheel?" Fynn directed, then stepped back to give space for William to take over. "Just keep her on that course and we won't hit Carcase," he said pointing to the compass bearing as Will's hands gripped the spoked timber wheel.

Except for a few course adjustment hints from Fynn to William, not much else was said over the remainder of the run down to Taylors. Both minds were evaluating what had been spoken of earlier.

As they entered inside passage of the island Fynn began to drop the sail. "We will use the motor to find a patch that we can fish. Kick her in the guts and when I have the sail down, then nudge her into gear," He ordered, in the same way he had heard some of the local fishermen say to their crew.

"Righto Captain," William humorously replied as he saluted while he turned the ignition key starting the motor.

On cue, William pushed the gear lever forward. *Amethyst* was now motoring slowly ahead.

"I'll take over from here – go to the bow and when I say 'let her go', pull the lever on the winch towards the stern, to drop the anchor," Fynn said as he spun the wheel to turn the vessel towards a patch he had spotted.

"OK – let her go" came the order as Fynn pulled the control into reverse, bringing the boat to a stop.

Fynn's timing of the anchor drop was perfect. *Amethyst* was sitting ideally over a white hole. Within minutes both blokes had their lines in the water, baited with squid that Fynn had purposely caught several days earlier.

"Had a bite," William called out, then he began to wind in his line "Flamin leather jacket," was his next remark as he hauled in a large blue coloured fish with a menacing dorsal spike.

Then Fynn followed. "Got a whack. Reckon it was a whiting, probably pinched my bait," and wound in his line at the same time as William was casting his out again.

Within a few seconds of Wills line hitting the bottom, he yelled excitedly "Got one!" then pulled in his line with not one, but two nice size Whiting glistening in the sunlight as they danced about on his suspended line.

"You beat me – not only with the first fish of the trip but then with the first whiting – and what makes it worst – a double header." Fynn joked as they gave each other a spontaneous high-five hand slap.

That was the moment of their bonding. The simple act of that high-five dissolved any apprehension between the two. The cloud of an emptiness in the boy's life was lifted. Fynn had found the father figure he hungered.

After a wonderful weekend of fishing and sailing and an overnight-stay moored in the shelter of Memory Cove, Fynn guided

Amethyst alongside the marina pontoon.

Helen had watched them sail across the bay and was waiting at the berth. She grabbed the forward line and tied it to the mooring cleat then scurried aft to accept the stern rope that William was holding out to her.

"How was your weekend Will? I hope Fynn didn't give you too many orders. He's a bit of a Captain when he is aboard and likes to run the ship his way." She said with an air of nervous excitement while tying that line to a cleat.

"Loved every minute – he's a real seadog, isn't he – best weekend I have had in ages," William replied from the deck as he gave Fynn a pat on the back.

"What about you Fynn – was it good for you as well?" Helen said as she stepped on board and gave both sailors a brief welcome-home hug.

"We had a great time, William is a good sailor. He surprised me when I saw he could steer a straight line. He must have been practicing. Guess what Mum??

Not only can he sail a yacht – he can catch fish as well! He landed the first fish of the day – on both days – but I caught the biggest whiting?" Fynn proudly stated as he opened the Esky to show off their catch.

That evening after the three enjoyed a meal of fresh caught crumbed Whiting, chips and coleslaw at the Britcher house, the time had come for a weary William to head for his home.

"I'll walk you to your car," Helen said to William.

"The sea air has knocked the stuffing out of me. I won't be long out of bed," he said as Helen opened the front door.

Just as Will's hand was about to reach for the car's door handle Helen took hold of his arm, positioned herself closer and said, "Thank you so much for spending time with Fynn. He really needed a Dad figure to share some time with him."

Before William was able to reply Helen softly kissed his cheek.

"I enjoyed every minute and hope to do it again sometime. Fynn and I get along well." He replied as he placed his hand on Helen's then reciprocated giving her hurried but affectionate kiss on her neck.

Helen returned inside and sat with Fynn in the lounge room. "I think he really is a nice person – what are your feelings now that the pair of you have spent time together?"

"Will's always been there for us, hasn't he?" then exaggerated his next word, 'and' – been there ever since I was born. He is almost a Dad, isn't he? This weekend we got to know each other. Yeh! He can be my Dad if you want him to," Fynn said as a big smile showed on his face.

"Slow down there Sonny-Jim. What are his feelings on the subject? By the way – do you realise, Will and I have never been on a proper date together – alone? What if he doesn't like me?" she said, wagging her fore-finger at Fynn.

"No chance of him not liking you," he joked back to his mother.

"What exactly do you mean by that?" she retorted.

"Even a blind man could see he definitely likes you – why can't you, Mum?"

"Until recently, I have never looked at him as anything more than a very, very good friend, but I have noticed that lately I seem to be touching and hugging him quite a lot."

Then as she gently rubbed her chin with the back of her fingers her voice tapered off after softly adding an involuntary,

"Hmmm, I wonder?"

A sudden epiphany stunned her. It was at this point it had become apparent to her, that apart from being comfortable with William, she too enjoyed his company and had begun to look forward to his visits.

In the ensuing months Helen and William spent more time together. On occasions Fynn was left to his own resources whilst the romancing pair went on weekend lunchtime soirees at restaurants in Tumby, Coffins and Mount Dutton Bay.

Knowing his mother had deposited a small amount of money from his father's estate in his bank account, Fynn began fantasizing about buying a boat of his own. One that he could venture further from the shore. A craft that would take him to the northern side of Boston Island or the 'Degei' wreck site on Donnington Island.

For weeks the nearing fifteen year old eagerly perused every available boating magazine and searched the internet in order to match himself with the best value and safest craft his modest funds could avail.

His dream had been answered when he saw the local boat dealership were advertising in the 'Times' newspaper, a second hand centre-console 5 metre fibreglass unit on a trailer with a fifty horse power motor, in stock and ready to go with all the equipment to meet marine safety standards.

"Going for a ride on my bike," Fynn's announced to his mother, next day after school.

"Where are going?" She asked.

"Just to get some hooks and sinkers from the boat shop," he offered as a partial truth hurriedly replied as he strapped on his safety helmet.

As soon as he had ridden out of the driveway he peddled furious towards to the boating business. His real intention of taking a look at the craft that had been advertised.

His heart raced at the very first view of the boat that had been aptly named *Nautical Buoy* neatly painted on the transom. 'This is the one for me,' he thought as he enthusiastically clambered aboard and held the wheel with one hand and put the other on the gear lever whilst looking towards the bow as if he was motoring along at sea. Fynn's rampant imagination was in top gear visualizing being out on the water skimming across the bay in his own runabout. His boyish fantasy came to an abrupt end a few minutes later when John the salesman, came over to talk with his potential client. While chatting he posed the question. "How is a young boy that is not yet sixteen and has only a bicycle, going to be able to get this boat to and from a boat ramp?"

Fynn knew that being reliant on his mother to be available every time he wanted to use the boat was not the answer. It was then the practicality of having something that was beyond his situation became obvious. His dream disintegrated. For several days his mood was subdued as he accepted the reality of having only the old ten foot tinny to go fishing in by himself. Although Fynn was capable of handling a big vessel such as their *Amethyst*, at his age it required two on board a runabout to be legal – one had to be over sixteen with a boat operator's license.

On cue, the seasonal calm days of autumn had arrived. Boston Bay was mill-pond smooth, the breeze was gentle. Helen and her good friend Kerrie were going to visit a school chum, now residing in the little town of Ungarra, some sixty kilometres north of Port Lincoln. Fynn had also been invited but declined.

Rather than spending a day listening to women chatting about school days and other gossip, he had other ideas about what he would prefer to be doing.

Britcher's family freezer supply of calamari had dwindled to almost nil. The seasonal squid had shifted away from Fynn's regular fishing spots, so the adventurous teen thought he might try his luck over the bay near Flinders Monument.

When fishing along the town's beaches, Fynn would normally row his small dinghy or allow it to drift over his fishing patches. The small two horse-power motor that was used on *Amethysts* inflatable had been at the mechanics to have the carburetor cleaned and was now in the house garage. Fynn was permitted to use a small motor on his tinny because of its low power and not able to exceed ten knots.

"Bit far to row to the Monument," Fynn mused as he picked up the light-weight motor to check if any fuel was in its tank. "Not much in there, that won't get me far – better get the fuel can and top it up," he said to himself.

Wearing his life jacket and with one arm loaded with a bucket of fishing tackle and the fuel container with what remained after topping up the tank. His other arm carrying the little engine, he headed down to Shelley Beach where the dinghy was stored, chained to a steel post above the high water mark. Within minutes Fynn had the motor securely mounted to the transom and the dinghy floating in the shallows. On the second pull on the starter cord, the motor sprang into life and the tinny and its skipper were soon heading east passing Snapper Rock on their way across the bay. Although not very powerful, the little motor manage to push the dinghy along at a slow yet steady rate when set at almost full throttle.

Sometimes squid can be illusive. Today was one such day. Fynn motored into the light breeze then drifted back downwind for almost half an hour before he landed his first catch.

As he pulled the ink-squirting squid aboard Fynn had a feeling he was being watched. His eyes scanned the shoreline to see if he could spot anyone.

A thought crossed his mind. "Perhaps it is a Fisheries Department officer." They would often hide in the bushes and observe the boats with their binoculars. Watching if anyone were keeping undersized fish or partaking in some other illegal activity.

"If it is the Fisheries they are doing a good job of concealment – can't see them," he assessed.

Starting at Stamford Hill Beach he worked his way to Wood Cutters Bay where his motor spluttered and died. A quick check of the fuel tank revealed it was empty.

Luckily he had brought along the extra fuel in the can. With refueling done, and quick tug on the starter cord the engine restarted and Fynn recommenced his drive-then-drift fishing.

At the beginning of the third drift, his back was hit with a substantial dousing of water. Turning around he saw the tail of a dolphin slide underwater.

"Must have been chasing a fish," he reckoned, and thought no more about the incident. After the next motor run he began another drift. Once again, when his back was turned he copped another soaking. Same thing, all he sighted was the tail of a dolphin heading downwards.

"Cut that out," he laughingly hollered in the direction of the unseen perpetrator.

Then another shower of water hit him from the opposite side to where he was looking. "Bloody hell – once an accident, then twice not an accident, but a third time is definitely deliberate. Show your face you cheeky bugger!" the now saturated Fynn called out.

He stood for a few minutes, looking around expecting his assailant to surface or soak him again.

In the distance Fynn spotted the rise and fall of a traveling dolphin's dorsal fin. "Nah, too far away – not him," he affirmed to himself.

Several more minutes lapsed without a sighting. Back to squidding. This time with great results.

Bang, bang, bang, he was hit with one squid after another in quick succession. So many that he filled his bag limit and had to call it a day.

Feeling very proud of himself he turned the boat towards home. Halfway through the journey the little motor once more began to splutter.

Immediately he assumed, "Must be out of fuel", then unscrewed the cap to check. The tank was still a quarter full of petrol.

After several pulls on the starter cord without successfully starting, other possibilities entered his thinking. "I bet the carby is blocked again – looks like I will have to start paddling."

Having to row home the next few kilometres never phased the young seaman. It was as natural as walking, to a lad that spent much of time in boats.

As he rowed he began daydreaming about the five metre runabout he hoped to have one day. Whilst pondering on the thought of being able to venture further and faster than in a little tinnie, his craft experienced a sudden surge of speed. "What the heck?" Fynn burst out, as he turned his head to look forward.

Tied to the bow was a short tether rope, which was previously dragging slackly alongside the hull. Something had pulled on it and was momentarily stretched ahead of the boat.

To Fynn's surprise, the rope went slack. Next, a dolphin rose to surface. Then, with its tail sent a huge splash of water directed at Fynn.

"You crazy bastard," he yelled at the mischief making mammal.

To his amazement the dolphin rose vertically out of the water and performed a tail walk for several metres, then dived headlong back into the sea. While it was doing the antic Fynn spotted a bright yellow tag pinned behind its dorsal fin.

Without another splashing session the very playful creature swam away. For the remainder of the trip home it was not to be seen again.

Late that afternoon William had called in to see Helen who had not yet arrived back home, when a rather weary young fisherman returned with his catch.

"G'day young fella, looks like you have a few in the bucket," said Will as Fynn trudged up the driveway lugging his catch in one hand and the motor balanced on his opposite shoulder.

"Yeh," the lad tiredly replied. "Bagged out with squid and now I will have to clean them."

"I'll give you a hand," Will enthusiastically volunteered.

"Hey William, have you ever seen a dolphin with a yellow dorsal tag," Fynn asked as he tipped the multi-tentacle critters on the cleaning bench.

"Sure did. The only one with a yellow tag, was a baby male and the very last one your father tagged when doing his study of the local dolphin pods. Reckon it would make him approximately three years older than you. I have only sighted him on a few occasions, always in the vicinity of the Spalding Cove and Horse Rock. He's quite friendly and often circles recreational fishing boats. People say it actually looks at who is in the boat, then swims away."

After Fynn had related his story of today's encounter, Will shook his head in amazement of the unique experience then remarked. "Pity you didn't have a video camera. It would have gone viral in the media," then stopped for a moment before adding in a serious tone. "So glad you had not recorded it – there would be dozens of idiots out there looking to see if they can find him. Keep it under your hat. Do not tell anyone, except your Mum perhaps?"

While waiting for the evening meal to finish cooking, Fynn retold his dolphin encounter to his mother.

"Mark – whoops, I mean your father, told me about how he helped save that dolphin when it had just been born. Evidently his mother had some difficulty during the birth. She was either too sore or perhaps too weak to lift her baby high up enough to get his first breath of air. Your dad was watching the birth, saw the little fellow was sinking, then dived in and hoisted him to the surface, held it there for a minute or two until it started to breathe. Every time your father went anywhere near the young'un and his mother, they would swim over to his boat. After a while the baby would come close enough for Mark to rub his back. He put that tag in the dolphins fin."

Then, as Helen served up the meal, she said earnestly to Fynn, "You do know that your looks are similar to your father's – perhaps he thinks you are Mark."

"Ya reckon?" he replied. "But that was years ago, how could

a dolphin remember for so long?"

"If your father was still with us, he could have answered that," Helen said as she placed his meal on the table.

With a freezer loaded with squid, and the troublesome motor in the mechanics workshop, Fynn had little desire to venture over to the Monument Beach area. However, images of the over-friendly dolphin doing his tail-walk trick dwelt in the back of his mind.

"Mum, if I had a bigger boat I could go to see that dolphin again," he said one morning at breakfast time.

"Speaking of bigger boats – did you know that William is going to buy one?" she informed Fynn then continued, "He told me that he was hoping to collect it from the dealer this week. Perhaps he may take us for a run on the weekend. I will suggest it on Friday evening when he visits."

With a cheeky beep-diddy-beep-beep on the car horn, William drove up the driveway as expected on Friday evening. As he entered the front door Fynn could see his smile was much broader than usual.

"Did you buy a boat – Mum said you were," Fynn quizzed as William went to Helen and gave her quick - I've-missed-you kiss – before answering.

"Sure did and it is a ripper. It's got everything. I had the dealer fit the latest fish-finder and map system, you would love it," he said with teasing delight.

"When do we get to see it? Helen asked.

"What are you two doing tomorrow? The forecast is good and I can't wait to see how it goes," he replied then added a proviso. "We won't be doing any fishing. It is just a shake down run for me to have a drive. Would one o'clock be suitable? That way we can be back here by tea-time,"

As one o'clock approached an excited Fynn positioned himself near the front widow. To his amazement William came walking up the road with no car, nor boat. "Hey Mum, Williams coming, but isn't driving – he's walking," he called out.

Helen moved to the front window to confirm what her son had said. Sure enough, he was walking.

Mother and son went out to greet him at the gate. "Where's your car and the boat?" they asked as he approached.

Before he could answer, Helen gave William a quick welcoming kiss.

"To cut a long story short I left it in a friends shed, not far from here. It won't fit in mine – have to shift some junk out first. Should have done that before I bought it. Are you ready to go, it's only a short walk."

"Fynn, you grab the lifejackets from the garage and I will get what we need from the house – won't be long Honey," Helen said without thinking.

Will smiled as he pondered on her word 'Honey'.

Within minutes the trio were walking towards his mates shed.

As they approached Helen questioned "Isn't this John's house, the bloke from the boat shop?"

"Yep," replied William as the shed door was being automatically lifted, to reveal John sitting in the driver's seat of William's car. A tarpaulin covered the boat on the trailer behind.

"Stand aside – I will drive her out," the salesman announced through his driver's side window.

The three obediently went and stood on the lawn area adjacent the paved drive. Helen asked "Why is a cover on the boat?"

"Keep the dust off," came Will's immediate reply.

John drove the rig out of the shed, turned off the motor and looked towards Will as he opened the car door at the same time calling out "You or me?"

William answered "You do it – I'll just watch!"

"What's that all about? Helen asked.

William replied with a huge grin on his face "It is my unveiling ceremony,"

"Suppose you will break a bottle of champagne over its bow as well," giggled Fynn, who was amused at all the fuss, at the same time wondering what the boat looked like.

John walked to the side of the boat, undid a rope that held down the tarp. With one hand he took hold of an edge of the cover, then turned and looked at the trio standing and waiting for the reveal of what was hidden under the tarp.

"Everybody – On the count of three." Spontaneously they joined in with the…"one, two, and three." Then John gave the cover a quick pull causing it to slide off and drape itself over the trailer mudguard.

Everyone cheered except Fynn. He was gob-smacked. "That's *Nautical Buoy*… that's the one I wanted," he forlornly stated.

"I know," said William. "I was in the shop looking for some plastic tubing for the laboratory when John told me about your visit. He explained how you said this was your perfect boat and how your heart sank when you realised it could never happen until you were sixteen and had your driver's license."

Fynn, unlike many other kids, was never jealous or possessive and was able to accept most situations. In this instance the joy of this occasion was slightly soured by discovering that William had purchased the very boat that he had searched for and dreamt to have.

"What's the matter mate, you don't look very happy," Will said as he walked towards the now obviously dejected lad.

"Perhaps this will cheer you up." He showed Fynn a bunch of keys with a small bright yellow miniature float attached.

"Take a look at what is written on the tag," William said as Fynn tentatively held out his left hand to accept them.

Fynn glanced down at the bunch, then flipped over the tag to read what was printed.

Stunned at what he was seeing, he stood motionless staring at the keys then began to sway his head back and forth and quietly muttered… "No way!"

As he raised his head to look at Will, an involuntary cascade of tears rolled down his face.

William broke Fynn's sudden reticence. "Come on pal, read out what it says, so your mother can hear."

More tears flowed from Fynn who was now desperately trying to stop the lump that was forming in his throat.

"If … If found …" he halted for a few seconds before he restarted in almost a whisper, "Return to owner." He paused again, took a deep breath then with quivering lips, finally reading in a louder voice, "Return to owner Fynn Britcher."

Will put his arm around the gob-smacked lad's shoulders. "She's all yours. Your name is also on her registration papers."

"Why?" the wet-eyed Fynn asked while glancing back and forth from his mother to William trying to seek an explanation.

Then Will offered as a vindication, "Your little tinny is a bit small for both of us and I would like to spend more time with you, doing what you like best."

He beckoned to Helen to stand close beside him. "And"…. before continuing, he put his other arm around her waist, turned to face towards her, then automatically they exchanged a kiss on the lips. Both heads turned to Fynn as they spoke in unison, "We would like your blessing for us to get married."

A huge smile erupted across Fynn's wet face as he wiped away tears with the back of his hand. "This is the best day ever. Not only do I get a boat, I will now have a Dad. What took you so long? It's a big yes from me," he cheekily replied as he gave them an endearing hug.

When James heard about the upcoming wedding, he immediately volunteered to be William's best man. The same as he had done years ago for his mate, Mark. Kerrie enthusiastically accepted her role to be Helen's bridesmaid. Julie's now teenage daughter Saffron jumped at the chance to be Helen's flower girl, while Fynn was allotted the task of carrying the rings.

Peter took on the job of being in charge of erecting the wedding ceremony bower, while the love of his life – Julie, would add her artistic touch with flowers and decorations that would adorn the eastern end of the lawned area of Mundy's Mooring. The Minister from St Thomas's who had performed Mark and Helen's wedding ceremony proudly accepted to be the celebrant for this marriage. Everything was set for their special day.

'Happy is the bride the sun shines on' – or so the adage goes. Helen was indeed elated when the wedding day was warm and sunny. Her days of being a single mother were now to end. William's heart was almost at bursting point after the years of waiting patiently, he was now to wed the woman of his dreams, the only woman he had ever loved. Fynn was over the moon with the realization he now had a 'dad'.

The ceremony flowed smoothly up to the point where the rings were to be exchanged. Fynn had mysteriously absented himself without anyone noticing.

"With these rings," announced the Minister in a much louder voice, then a hush went through the assembly.

"Where's Fynn – he was supposed to present the rings?" the puzzled flower girl Saffron, said as she looked among the guests.

The splashing of a swimmer coming ashore on the beach flanking the procedure suddenly drew everyone's attention.

It was Fynn, still fully clothed and soaking wet in his suit and tie holding a glass bowl filled with seawater above his head.

As he approached the bridal group the Minister winked at Fynn then announced "We are now to have a special ceremony included in this wedding."

Helen and Will looked at each other with puzzlement as to what he was implying.

The dripping wet Fynn passed the bowl of water to the preacher who returned a sneaky smile and followed by an acknowledging nod to him.

"Today," the Minister stated to the crowd holding forth the bowl as if were a chalice. "Today we add another element to this marriage. That is the receiving of rings and the acknowledgement of the sea that surrounds Port Lincoln. In this family union it has always been the inclusion in their lives and their family's lives – the sea. On this special occasion, we give thanks to a sea that has provided employment, sustenance, knowledge and recreation. I now ask Helen and William to hold out and join their hands together to accept the waters that flow through their lives and their wedding bands."

The Preacher returned the bowl to Fynn then said in a prayer-like tone – "To all present, we bear witness of our respect for the life-giving sea and the acceptance of these rings. Amen," after which he gave Fynn a sign to begin to pour the water through the couple's outstretched fingers.

Still stunned by the inclusion of this ceremony in their sacrament, they noticed that Fynn's face was full of delight as he poured the water until the rings dropped into their hands.

Magically, Helens ring fell into Williams hand and his into hers.

The Minister then put forward both of his hands and laid them over the bride and grooms hands to cover their golden bands.

A few seconds passed before he lifted his hands then said solemnly "William and Helen please place the rings on each other's fingers and repeat 'I thee wed' as you do so."

The wet rings easily slid over their knuckles, then the smiling couple looked towards the preacher as he gave his next instruction.

"You are now man and wife – William and Helen Scott. Please confirm your love for each other with a kiss."

The gathering of guests erupted into applause. Not only for the happy couple but also for the uniqueness of the seawater inclusion in the ceremony, a ritual not ever seen before.

The newlyweds, bridal party and Minister turned to face their audience for a 'photo moment'.

William smiled towards the cameras then turned to Fynn, "You never fail to amaze me. That was a beautiful gesture. It was planned so well – neither you nor the Minister gave any hint to what you were going to do."

The Minister chipped in, "It was all Fynn's idea, and he deserves the credit. My part, was to continue as if it was going to be an ordinary ceremony! Fynn awoke my understanding of how great an influence the sea has on our lives, especially for this family. Paying homage to the sea was a natural inclusion."

Mark then wrapped his arms around the sodden Fynn.

"Son, yes I can now call you Son – I admire the way you think and most of all – I love you."

"Love you too – 'Dad', responded a now exceptionally happy Fynn.

For the now family of three, *Amethyst* was the forefront of many weekend voyages exploring more of the offshore islands much to the delight of William who, apart from his trip to Memory Cove with Fynn, had not seen much of the coast due to his shore bound laboratory work. Nothing out of the ordinary occurred on these trips. However on one occasion, as they sailed past Dangerous reef to see its colony of large Sea Lions, William was not impressed with the strong odour of a mixture of bird and seal excrement that wafted through the air.

"That stink makes me want to puke," he exclaimed as he almost vomited. So for his sake, rather than linger in the vicinity to watch the seals, they sailed onward to Thistle Island. Here they stayed the night in the deep crystal clear water of Whalers Bay where a family of shiny black New Zealand fur seals gathered on the rocks (without the odour of the reef colony).

A few weeks a later trip to Spilsby Island, then over to the marina at Tumby Bay, where they tied up for another overnight camp in order to catch up with some of Helen's old school friends and share a meal at the Sea Breeze Hotel.

There were also times when the 'men only' would take Fynn's runabout, *Nautical Buoy* on short fishing trips. One evening after William had finished his work Fynn said "Let's go to the Le-Hunte Shoal marker beacon in the bay. Might hook on to a snapper or two. We can launch the runabout from Stenross boat ramp, it will be closer than the Billy Lights ramp."

Immediately after they had dropped anchor close to the big black pole with its flashing light at the top. Will asked, as he threaded a squid head on his hook, "How did you find out about this spot."

"A nice old bloke, I think they call him the Dutchman or something like that, told me when I helped him drag his dinghy over the sand and carry his oars back to his car – reckoned he was getting too ancient to fish anymore. He also said to catch snapper we had to be patient, not making any sound, or shine a light in the water that would scare the fish. Our lines have to be baited and in the water as the sun begins to set – this was the best time to catch the big reds."

The 'men' sat without any further conversation watching the sun creep slowly behind Winters Hill. Then, just as the sun disappeared as if on cue, 'Click', then another protracted 'click-click' went the ratchet on Williams reel. "Wait," whispered Fynn, "Wait till it takes more line then pull on the rod to set the hook in its mouth." After another two slow clicks, the line went loose.

"What now?" an anxious but controlled Will, quietly asked

with his hand on the rod ready to strike.

"Get ready – it's picked up the bait," Fynn replied still in a whisper, his eyes glued on the loose line. "Now – pull!!" he announced loudly.

William yanked back his rod just as the line went taut. His reel began to scream as he fumbled to reset the drag to begin the fight with what he hoped was a red-scaled opponent.

This began William's battle to land whatever it was on the end of his line in the deep ink-black water.

After a ten minute tussle, Will heard the words he wanted to hear, "I see colour – it's a snapper," Fynn was excited as he grabbed the landing net and poised himself ready to collect the fish.

"About seven to eight kilo's – not bad" exclaimed Fynn leaning over to hoist the fish aboard. Then whoosh, a big spray of sea water hit him in the side of his face. This was not caused by the fish that was now held tight in the net – it came from the tail of a something much larger.

"I bet it's that cheeky dolphin again," Fynn spluttered as he landed the fish on to the deck. "I thought dolphins slept at night – don't they?"

As William bent down to remove the hook from the snapper's mouth, "In your father's notes I read something about dolphins only taking a nap for a couple of hours each day. Seems that 'friend' of yours has been watching you again."

Immediately after William finished his sentence, Fynn's 'friend' did another tail-walk close to the stern of the boat.

"Wow! – Now I have seen it all. A wild dolphin that can do tricks – bloody amazing!" Will said shaking his head.

"The bugger has probably scared all the other fish away. Anyway, we have got enough fish – this one should feed us for a few days. Time to go home," Fynn suggested as he pressed the anchor winch button.

While motoring out of the darkness of the bay towards the sodium orange lights of the Stenross boat ramp, Fynn's 'splash perpetrator' could be seen in the glow of the green starboard navigation light, following alongside.

"That dolphin has a fixation on you. He seems able to recognise your face. Perhaps it is like your mother said weeks ago – You look so much like your father."

As their boat turned past the grey granite rock breakwater and idled toward the ramp pontoon, a rather agitated woman who had been standing at the top section, came rushing down and approached questioning them, "Did you see a dinghy when you came in? My son was due back before dark and that was an hour ago."

Rather than tie the boat to a pontoon bollard, William held the craft alongside with his hands then asked the lady, "Do you know which in direction he went?"

"He said he was going to fish for squid from here to Boston House. He can't have gone far just rowing."

The instant she finished saying that, Fynn copped a quite unexpected shower of water from his dolphin 'friend'.

"No time for your weird sense of fun," he chastised the splasher. "We have to go and look for her son."

Fynn re-started the motor as William pushed the craft away from the pontoon.

"There is a powerful torch in the side pocket under the bow," Fynn stated as he slowly edged the throttle forward.

After a short rummage through the bits and pieces, William found the torch and switched it on.

"Wow, that is one very bright beam," he exclaimed as he

swung the torch back and forth along the shoreline towards the 'Oasis' plus an occasional brief scan out to sea, hoping to sight the lost fisherman.

In the light he spotted Fynn's dolphin slapping the surface with its tail about 80 metres out from the shore. Staying on the surface it did several low rolls on to its side. Each time with one pectoral fin pointing in the same direction.

"Reckon your mate is trying to attract our attention and tell us something – maybe he wants you to steer the boat the way he is indicating," Will suggested.

"Or he is just being stupid," replied a skeptical Fynn.

"It won't hurt to look, the breeze might have blown the dinghy out into the bay," William recommended as he scanned slightly ahead of the Bottlenose 'friend' that was now swimming towards the North Entrance.

With the boat slowly motoring along around 5 knots, both pair of eyes were glued to the illuminated area of water.

"I think I can see it – bring your light a little more to Port. Yep, there he is," a relieved Fynn said as he turned his craft towards a rather forlorn looking lad sitting in the almost submerged hull of a small alloy dinghy.

"Thank heavens you found me or I would have had to sit in this until morning, it's too far from the shore for me to swim," grumbled the hapless young fisherman in the torch light. His teeth were beginning to chatter with the cold.

Fynn's first question was "What happened?"

The lad replied as William held *Nautical Buoy* alongside the floundering dinghy, "Drain plug must have come loose and fell out. If it wasn't for the flotation under the seats she would have completely sunk. The battery for the lights must have shorted out – it's dead. My paddles and my bag of safety gear floated away as I was trying to stop the water from entering. I should have tied them in."

Following Fynn's instructions, William attached a tow line to the bow of the little tinnie, then secured the loose end to a stern cleat of *Nautical Buoy.*

"We will tow you in. Sit at the stern to keep the bow up. As we travel the water should drain out through the hole it came in. When it does, I want you to lean over and put this spare drain plug in the socket," Fynn ordered with his usual skipper-like authority as he passed his spare drain plug over.

Steadily, Fynn began to tow the dinghy towards the now distant lights of the boat ramp. At first the dinghy wallowed from side to side until Fynn adjusted his speed to lift the dinghy's bow. The water began to drain exactly as Fynn had predicted. It wasn't long before the tinny was almost empty of its saline burden. With the spare bung reinserted, they were soon within a few hundred metres of the boat ramp and a very relieved mother.

With a priority to get the young fellow and his boat to safety, there was little concern as to the whereabouts of the guiding dolphin. His role in the rescue had been quickly forgotten.

Back at home William proudly boasted to Helen how 'they' had rescued the lad and his dinghy, emphasizing Fynn's seamanship skill, knowing exactly what to do to get the lad and his water-filled boat back to safety. Then, like many fishermen, gave a slightly exaggerated summary of how 'he' had fought hard to land the snapper. Followed by an account of Fynn's dolphin 'mate' antics. At this point he remembered how their aquatic water-splashing friend had alerted the pair to what direction they should concentrate their search.

"Thanks to Fynn's dolphin buddy we were able to locate the young lad. He must have known that boy was in trouble," then added, "If only dolphins could speak, he might have said – What about me? Have you forgotten it was this crazy dolphin that guided you to the boy's dinghy?"

Helen pointed a finger towards a framed charcoal sketch of Mark that her arty friend Julie had drawn many years ago.

"Mark often said we have heaps more to learn from these extremely intelligent creatures. That's exactly what he would say, If only they could speak?"

Then she asked her son, "Have you decided on a name for your friendly Dolphin pal?"

"Mmmm?" pondered Fynn, "There is already a 'Flipper' that is famous, so that rules out using my father's nickname 'Flippers'.

"How about calling him Splash," William suggested.

"Great name – that would make a terrific dolphin name, especially for that one!" Fynn replied.

Within a few short weeks the chilled winds of winter dominated the weather patterns. Both *Amethyst* and *Nautical Buoy* lay idle awaiting better conditions.

Fynn did the occasional trip to Fisheries Bay with some school friends to do some surfing on the days when a decent swell was rolling in.

One Saturday morning at breakfast Helen said, "The weather forecast stated today was going to be nice and sunny. I hear there is some good sets on Left Point. How about we all go surfing and have a picnic on the beach today?"

Fynn laughed. "Mum, it has been years since you waxed a

board and went surfing. The water will be cold and you will have to wear a wetsuit. I bet your old wettie doesn't fit you anymore!"

"Would you like to put money on that? For your information, I tried on one of my old summer dresses yesterday and it fitted perfectly – just as my wetsuit will."

Then William pipped in "One in, all in – we are a family now! However I must tell you that I have never been surfing in my life – you'll have to teach me."

"That's a job for you Mum. Both of you can ride the shore breaks and I'll surf Left Point."

"Brilliant idea Fynn! We have an old wettie that Willy can wear and I would love to teach him," Helen said as she reached out and affectionately held William's hand.

A picnic lunch was packed and a pair of dusty vinyl bags that held Helen's beloved older-style long Malibu boards were taken from their rack in the garage and loaded onto the car, along with Fynn's much shorter board.

As they drove past Tulka and the entrance to the Lincoln National Park, William was noticeably silent until they were adjacent the landlocked waters of Sleaford Mere, then he raised his concerns. "Are there any sharks at Fisheries?"

"Sometimes," replied Fynn.

"What do I do if I see one?" Will posed the question.

"Keep your feet up and catch the first available wave back to the shore," Fynn quipped then gave a little chuckle before he continued. "There were possibly more sharks at Dangerous Reef and Thistle Island waiting to have meal of seal. You did not seem to have any fear then."

"Yeh but, I was on *Amethyst* and not in the water there,"

exclaimed the nervous Will.

Helen then explained to her husband. "If you learn how to stay on your board you will be alright. That is – if a shark doesn't take a chunk out of your board," she giggled.

"You both certainly know how to scare a bloke, perhaps I might stay on the beach and watch you two surf," suggested William.

At Fisheries, Helen drove along the rough stony track to Left Point. Will untied the short board while Fynn slipped on his neoprene suit.

"See you both back at beach at lunchtime," Fynn shouted over his shoulder as he began to scramble down the stony cliff-face. At the water's edge he stood for a minute observing the wave patterns, and couple of other people surfing then launched himself into the emerald-green water. Helen and Will lingered for a while to watch their son easily grab his first wave, surf it like a professional, then paddle out again to wait for another set.

On the gleaming white sand of the Fisheries Beach, Will apprehensively pulled on his wet suit. After Helen's short lesson of how to paddle and stand up on his board, he timidly followed her into the chilly crystal clear water.

Laying on his belly, paddling out was easy. Next came his many unsuccessful attempts to catch one of the half-metre high shore-break waves. On his sixth try, Willy finally manage to be propelled forward by a wave. His endeavor to stand ended rapidly. After a few metres he lost his balance causing the board to shoot out from under. Not to be beaten, he tried several more times. Helen was easily surfing every wave that she decided to tackle. Finally a very exhausted William managed to ride a wave.

Helen stood on her board and clapped her hero. "Bravo," she shouted as he passed. It was then she noticed a dark object swimming directly at him.

Calmly she called to William to keep going into the shore. Her unsuspecting hero gave the thumbs up as he wobbled his way toward the beach.

Helen followed close behind. When they reached the shallow water, Helen stood looking out into the bay.

"What are you looking for," Will quizzed her.

"Not sure if it was a dolphin or a big bitey I saw before we came in," she confessed.

"You mean – I was in the water with something that may have eaten me for lunch?" he said as he quickly headed for dry sand, leaving the board to float in on its own accord.

"There it is – over there – look," she shouted as her outstretched arm pointed in its direction. Then the dark object leapt out of the water. "Dolphin – it's a dolphin," she said with relief.

"Dolphin or not, I am not going back in," said William as he beckoned for Helen to un-zip the back of his wetsuit.

Fynn was surfing much further out than his parents. As he slid off one wave that took him closer in, he noticed his patents walking across the sand towards the car. Presuming this was now lunchtime he caught the next decent wave and surfed towards the beach. It took only that one well-chosen wave to travel the distance. As he surfed shoreward he could see in the glass-clear water, a dolphin following closely alongside. With one eye constantly watching Fynn and with barely a flick of its tail his companion skimmed effortlessly along, propelled by the inertia of the wave staying with him until the water became shallow. Then with a quick backflip headed out to sea.

"Did you see that?" Fynn shouted to William as he ran up the beach carrying his board. "There was a dolphin surfing with me and it followed me all the way in."

"Did it have a yellow tag?" Helen asked.

"No it wasn't 'Splash', it was just another wild dolphin, However I did noticed it had a large nick out of its dorsal fin," he replied.

"Perhaps we should start calling you the Fynn the Dolphin King. They seem to deliberately seek you out," William said as he passed him a towel.

"Why would they do that?" Fynn asked.

"I have no idea why. Maybe that one came from a group your father was studying and mistook you for him."

A few minutes after they had finished snacking on the contents of the hamper, grey clouds began to replace the blue sky. The air temperature was dropping rapidly as the wind had turned more southerly.

"We should call it a day and head for home," Will announced as he threw the remaining food scraps to an audience of hungry seagulls that had positioned themselves ready to scavenge any morsel that might come there way.

"No need to stay and shiver. Might as well go home," Helen said shaking the sand from her hands before repacking the picnic basket.

"That was your first surfing lesson, you did well honey. Perhaps after a few more lessons you will be out there with Fynn, tackling the big waves."

William replied, "If that was a hungry shark and not a dolphin out there – I would never go surfing again."

He then turned towards Fynn, "I'd like to think that dolphin was there to protect us. It is often said – when dolphins are in the area there will be no sharks. However the theory has not yet been fully proven, so don't rely on it."

The forthcoming year was a time for Fynn to start his final year at the Port Lincoln High School. Being future-minded he had decided on attending university to gain a degree in Marine Science as did all his parents, His paternal father Mark, mother Helen and his now father William had all gained their Degrees. Hence Fynn was determined to achieve his aim and diligently put his school work ahead of having fun.

Apart from an occasional evening fishing to replenish the family freezer or the day trip to one of the coasts surf beach with his friends, much of his time was now being devoted to study.

As he neared the end of term three, Fynn became a tad restless. His mind would drift. His thoughts were those of being aboard *Nautical Buoy*, exploring the nearby islands and reefs or motoring around the bay looking for 'Splash'. His waning concentration had not gone unnoticed by his mother and she thought it best to discuss the matter with William.

"Fynn desperately wants to gain good marks to qualify for Uni. Have you any idea of what we can do for him to get his mojo back on track," she asked.

"*Amethyst* has been tied up for the last few months. Perhaps we should all take a trip to somewhere exciting. I am sure he will come back refreshed and get back into his study. Grab a map of the Gulf and let's see where we might sail," William suggested.

Helen unquestioningly went to the library and returning, laid the map on the dining room table.

"Over the years I have visited most of the islands in Spencer Gulf. The only one that Fynn has not been to, is Wedge," she said as she pointed to its location on the chart where it was marked as Gambier Islands. "We call it 'Wedge' due to its shape. Gambier is the official name but no one uses it except for the little island north of Wedge. That we refer to as North Gambier."

Thrusting his thumb upwards to signify his assent William enthusiastically responded, "Gambier Island – Wedge whatever it is! I have never been there either, so it will be another adventure for us men. The October long weekend is in a fortnight, we can stay for two days."

With the wind on her nose, the journey to Wedge was relatively slow. *Amethyst* had to battle a brisk southerly that lifted salty spray over the bow the entire distance, much to the delight of Fynn. He relished the experience of tacking back and forth across the wind and the course changes that were required for her to travel without using the motor.

"Ready to go about," he would shout before he altered course to make the tack, then call for William to winch the sheet as the boom swept over their heads. Being a new experience for William he valued the lesson of how to zig-zag sail close to the wind.

In the lee of the island the wind dropped noticeably, the water calmed and the warmth of the afternoon sun soaked through their body. The main was lowered and the engine started as they cruised eastward along the white sandy beach of the northern side to select the perfect anchorage for the night. *Amethysts* anchor was dropped in sight of a windmill that stood behind the low sand dune near the far eastern end.

"Whiting or Sweep for tea?" Fynn asked. At first Helen requested they have whiting. However William reckoned that a nice fresh Sweep would make a delightful change to having the often consumed Whiting.

Helen tentatively agreed to his conjecture as she passed him a fishing rod. "Sweep you want – then Sweep you must catch," she said cheekily smiling at him.

Fynn said as he took the rod from William "You won't catch one here, no rocks, only sand. I'll take the inflatable and catch a few off the point."

Then he answered Williams' request of going in the dinghy with him, "Sorry Dad no room – you stay onboard and help Mum prepare the salads."

As Fynn motored the little craft towards the rocky point William said to Helen, "If he hasn't been here before – how does he know where to catch Sweep?"

"He's a clever cookie. Somehow he stores in his brain every story he has been told about where to catch what type of fish. A bloke named Ken who often fished this area, once told him how delicious it was to eat fresh-caught pan-fried sweep. That was ten years ago, Fynn was just five and he still remembers the places where Ken said he caught his sweep."

Will stepped down into the cabin "I had better get the binoculars and keep an eye on him – just in case a big Noah thinks of having him for his tea. Not only does he have a good memory, seems to have little fear of being by himself on the water."

"You really care about him, don't you?" Helen said as he passed the binoculars up from below.

"If I ever had a son," he said then paused momentarily to adjust the binoculars then began again, "If I ever had a son – that is exactly like I would love him to be – just like Fynn."

"You do have a son, and he is just like the one you spoke of, and he has a father just like the one he always wanted" Helen said as she wrapped her arms around her husband.

Only half an hour had passed before Fynn's playful voice called out – "Ahoy there me hearties. Put the pan on the stove," as he tied the inflatable alongside *Amethyst.* "Got dinner for us – three nice sweep; as ordered!" then clambered aboard.

"The rock-cod gave me hell but I outsmarted them. I chucked in a squid head to keep them busy while I caught the sweep." He proudly held up each fish one at a time to show off his catch.

"Dad, I caught 'em but you will have to scale and gut 'em, then Mum can coat the lot with breadcrumbs. We will have the feast of kings. The freshest fish one can ever eat," he said as he handed a knife to a rather bemused William.

"Perhaps one not as cheeky," Will said with a wink and looking knowingly at Helen.

She giggled, "Yep, I agree with that."

"What are you two on about?" Fynn asked with a puzzled look on his face.

"Private joke," his mother replied then she winked back at William as he set about scaling the pan sized fish.

In the warm evening air the three were sitting on the deck of *Amethyst.* Each with a plate of food on their lap, the trio dined on Fynn's catch. Helen raised her glass of chilled white wine, "That was certainly a team effort. One to catch, one to clean and the other to cook. Well done everyone. Cheers!"

To which William replied, "I'll drink to that – we are a great team. This fish tastes better than I could have ever imagined. I definitely made the right choice!"

"My turn," Fynn said raising again his glass of apple juice. "What more could I ever want? Here we are on board anchored at Wedge. Perfect meal, plus I have the best Mum in the world and I have an amazing Dad. Love you both. Here's to a perfect day with many more to follow. Cheers!"

"Love you too" Will and Helen replied in unison.

Early next morning as the sun began its golden journey from behind the horizon, the crew onboard *Amethyst* awakened. A gentle breeze made only a slight ripple on the water. Overhead an Osprey glided high above, following the shoreline in search of a fish breakfast.

"It is my turn to prepare a meal. Fruit juice and toast for everyone!" William chuckled as he set three glasses and plates on the galley table and slipped four slices of bread onto the stoves griller tray.

"Don't go to a lot of trouble – will ya!" Fynn replied cheekily as he pulled his tee-shirt over his head.

"Son, it will be a light breakfast first – then a sumptuous lunch of fresh fish, that your mother and I will catch and this time you will cook," Will answered.

"That's if you catch some. If you don't – a can of baked beans that I will cook to perfection – just for you," Fynn laughingly boasted as he poured himself a tumbler of orange juice.

"Where is mine?" Helen said as Fynn was about to take a

drink from his glass while she switched on the ship to shore radio then announced. "Coastal weather report will be on in a minute, let's hope it is all good so we can stay another day."

Within a few minute a voice came over the radio –'*Good morning, this is MVR channel 88 with the Port Lincoln coastal area weather report for today. No warnings have been issued. The forecast is for a south-westerly swell of 1 to 2 metres with light westerly breezes of 5 knots in the morning then swell increasing to 2 to 3 metres and winds freshening to 10 to 15 knots in the afternoon'*.......

"That's what I was hoping to hear, the morning sounds all good. We can give the east side of North Gambier a try. We will be in the lee all day," said Helen.

"Old Ken told me he caught some whopper whiting there, not far from the Osprey nest. And he also said, if we are in too close the Rock Cods will rip our baits off. All we have to do is find the nest and fish out from there," spoken like an authority on the location by Fynn.

Immediately after breakfast the anchor was winched aboard. With only the jib set, *Amethyst* slid along at a gentle pace towards the Island.

"This is what I call paradise," William said as he sat sunning himself with his arms outstretched across the back rest of his deck seat. "What we should do, is go on a month-long sail up the Gulf to Cowell, Whyalla and Port Augusta then back home on the other side – Port Pirie and Wallaroo." He mused so that everyone could hear.

"I'll be in that," said Fynn as he steered the yacht.

"And – who is going to do our work for us while we are away?" Helen taunted.

"A bloke can only dream," came William's reply.

"Righto son, where are these big Whiting you were told we might catch," William asked as they neared the vicinity of the nest, then placed a half frozen squid bodies on the bait board to cut ready for their hooks .

After a few minutes of scanning the island's shore, William was first to spot the Osprey's eerie. "There it is!" he said as he pointed to a pile of sticks high up on the cliff face.

Immediately Fynn released the self-furl on the jib to allow the boat to come to a slow stop.

"Might try a drift first and if we find a patch then we will drop the pick," came his confident skipper-like command.

Within a few minutes both parents had their lines baited and in the water. *Amethyst* drifted slowly parallel to the island.

"Got one!" shrieked Helen excitedly as she wound in her catch. "Rock Cod" laughed Will, adjusting the rudder position.

"To make things worse, it has swallowed the hook right down," Helen said in disgust.

"I'll get it out," said Fynn as he grabbed hold of Helen's flapping catch.

Unfortunately for the fish, the hook was embedded deep in its gills and was bleeding profusely.

"One for the crabs to eat," Fynn said as he flung the fish back into the water, where it floated around on the surface.

Then suddenly – Whoosh!

An Osprey swooped from above with talons outstretched, snapped up the hapless fish, and then flew off with its catch securely held in its razor sharp claws.

With their mouths agape all three watched as the bird rose effortlessly to its nest of sticks on the overlooking craggy cliff-face.

"Wow! See that – that was fantastic," shouted an ecstatic Fynn.

As the boat drifted further out, William went below to get the binoculars.

"Two chicks," he exclaimed as he scanned the nest through the lenses.

"Next Rocky we catch will be for the babies," said an eager Fynn ready to begin fishing, then casting his line with the hope of hooking another one.

"Fish on," yelled Helen as she struggled to wind in her catch.

"You've done a William," chuckled Fynn as he peered over to observe what his mother had on her line before announcing. "It's a double-header Whiting,"

Within a minute Fynn was also pulling in a nice Whiting as William hurriedly cast his line with the binoculars still swinging around his neck.

"Fish on here too," William declared as he landed a huge whiting. "Now that is what I call a beauty," he said, proudly holding aloft his catch for the others to see.

Not to be out-done Helen landed another one of similar size.

"Amazing," she said, "Here we are trying to catch a Rock Cod for the babies, instead we are hauling in Whiting. Start the motor Fynn and take her in closer."

Amethyst was now within fifty metres of the shore – a guaranteed spot to haul in Rock Cod. William was first to get a bite – "Got ya," he exclaimed and began to wind in his line.

About the sixth crank of his reel his line went tighter, more than just having a fish on the end. The drag on his reel began to screech. "Must have something more than a rocky," he panted as he tried in vain to crank the handle of his reel. William struggled to maintain his grip on the now seriously bending rod.

"Don't rush it – just keep enough pressure on to hold the hook in place. Not sure what it is, you will have to tire it out before you will get it alongside," came wise words from the experienced Fynn. For the next ten minutes William puffed and strained as he fought to keep whatever it was from breaking his line. Eventually the fish became less aggressive and responded to his effort to haul in the line.

"I can see it," called an excited Helen. "It's a bloody big Kingie,"

Fynn grabbed the gaff and held it over the side, waiting for the fish to come within his reach.

William's big fish had almost ceased it fight and flapped about weakly on the surface. As he guided his catch closer to the boat Fynn leaned further out to gaff the fish.

"Watch out – Shark!!!" yelled Fynn as he jumped away from the side.

Suddenly there was an explosion of water as a huge grey shape with cavernous, teeth-filled jaws had rocketed up from below and grabbed the unfortunate kingfish. William's line tightened for a moment then went slack. He could now only watch his once in a lifetime catch disappear into the deep emerald green water in the mouth of a two and half metre juvenile Great White.

"Wow – that was a close one, it could have ripped my arm off," Fynn announced with a touch of bravado as he replaced the gaff in the gunwale clip.

William had now turned pale and sat shaking on the deck trying to comprehend the event.

Then with a slight tremble in his voice softly said, "Wasn't expecting that! Fifteen minutes of struggle, and a bloody big 'Pointer' pinches my fish. Just goes to show how quick a shark attack can happen."

"That's the food chain in action as very few have ever seen," said Helen then continued. "You catch a small fish and it gets eaten by a bigger one then a much larger predator makes a meal of both them. Don't worry honey – just think of the story you can tell everyone," Helen said as she put her arms around her stressed hero, then suggested "I reckon it is time to head back to Lincoln."

"Well I'm not giving up – I am going to catch a rock cod for the babies before we go," Fynn stated as he cast his line. "The shark has probably scared them off, but it is worth a try, just to watch the mother bird snatch another fish from the water.

Contrary to his doubts about fish being scared off by the shark, it wasn't long after his sinker hit the bottom a fish jerked the line.

"Mum, get the camera ready – I have got one," he said as he fast-cranked his reel to ensure his catch was landed before something else could grab it.

With a quick flip of the rod a hapless Rock Cod was landed on the deck.

The well embedded hook took a few seconds to remove. Fynn then held the fish high above his head, waving it back and forth to attract the attention of the Osprey.

From the cliff face the sharp sighted bird launched itself into the air. With barely a flick of its outstretched wings, it was soon circling the boat with eyes fixated on Fynn and the fish.

"Are you ready Mum – here it comes," he called, then tossed the fish as far out as he could.

Click, click, click went the shutter of Helen's digital camera as the bird swooped in with forward poised talons and seized the fish from the surface.

"Now that's something every kid should get to see," said William watching the huge bird return to its nest with the fish dangling in its claws, while Helen continued to follow it's movements with her camera.

Helen changed the lens on her camera.

"Going to get a few shots feeding the chicks," she stated, adjusting the focus while aiming her camera at the nest.

Once again her camera clicked away taking another dozen frames of the bird in its natural habitat.

Helen scrolled through the shots on the camera screen. "Yep, got a couple of nice ones," then said to Fynn as she packed her camera back in its protective bag, "Let's get underway and head for home, I think we have had enough excitement for today."

Being a good deckhand, William proceeded to tidy up and stow the fishing gear in the locker. Fynn started the motor then pointed the boat northwards to clear the island.

With Gambier now well astern of *Amethyst*, Helen busied herself cooking a feast of fresh whiting while William stood silent next to 'the skipper' Fynn as they voyaged home. For several minutes he was mesmerised by the rise and fall of the boat's bow as it sliced through the water.

Without taking his eyes off the sea he said sincerely "This is my dream come true. A beautiful wife a wonderful son and the privilege of spending time together out here on the sea and being able to see the natural real world, not just the wall inside of a laboratory. Then to top that off with having a close encounter with a shark." He transferred his gaze toward Fynn, "Life is good, and I am a very lucky man."

Fynn smiled and answered. "I too have the best Mum ever and a really great Dad. Couldn't ask for more."

"This is 'Volunteer Marine Rescue' radio calling all vessels in the vicinity of Dangerous Reef" crackled through the cabin speakers.

Then repeated the message, *"VMR 88 calling all vessels in the vicinity of Dangerous Reef"*

Helen quickly responded, *"Amethyst* to VMR we are east of Dangerous, how can we assist?"

"VMR to Amethyst – Had a request from a vessel needing assistance near the Reef. Vessel reported it is having engine problems – Can you assist?"

"Roger – Can do," replied Helen.

"VMR to Amethyst – Vessel is at anchor 500 metres north of the reef. Please confirm when you get there."

"Amethyst to VMR – Roger, got that, 500 metres north – *Amethyst* out."

"VMR to Amethyst – will maintain listening watch – VMR out."

Before Helen could say anything the ever alert Fynn had altered course and was heading towards the stricken vessel.

William once again took the binoculars out of their case and scanned the area. "Fynn, I can just see a boat slightly more North of where you are traveling." Without saying a word Fynn immediately altered his course while concentrating on the white spot in the distance.

Fifteen minutes later the boat could be seen clearly. A man and a young dark haired girl were frantically waving what appeared to be towels, in the direction of *Amethyst.*

Fynn guided *Amethyst* close to the broken down boat, then called out "What's your problem?"

"Motor won't start," came the reply from the man on board.

"Is it turning over?' shouted Fynn.

"Yep – got plenty of battery power but she just won't start," he replied

"How's your fuel situation," William called out.

"Half a tank according to the gauge," came the answer.

"Do you want me to come aboard and take a look," Fynn asked

"Yes, please."

Fynn said to William "I will pull alongside, and get the bloke to pass us a rope. We will tie it to our midship cleat. Then get him to tie his end to their stern cleat. Then I'll jump across and tie another rope to their bow. Better put half dozen fenders over the side to protect the hulls."

After outlining his plan to the unfortunate boat owner, Fynn skillfully maneuvered *Amethyst* closer and eased her against the much smaller boat. William tied off the stern rope as Fynn jumped the metre wide gap to the fibreglass half-cabin boat, then quickly secured the forward line.

Both vessels danced in the low swell that was running past the reef area. William's job was to prevent either boat slamming against each other and held a larger fender in position ready to prevent any hull damage.

"By the way – I'm Rick and this is my daughter Michelle," the man said as he readied himself for a handshake.

"I'm Fynn," then held out his hand towards the man for the shake, but with his eyes on the young girl.

Fynn was bought back to attention when, Thump!! The two boats banged against each other. "Sorry! Wasn't expecting that one," called out William as he adjusted the location of the fender.

"Better have a squizzy and see what the problem is," Fynn affirmed, then asked Rick to try and start the motor.

After three attempts the motor failed to fire up, so Fynn asked "Where is the fuel tank?"

"It's under the floor," the man replied then began to pull back the matting that covered the deck hatch.

Fynn lifted the retainer catch, open the hatch to expose the long stainless steel tank. Kneeling down he reached for the fuel cap.

As he screwed the cap loose, a sucking sound was heard as air rushed into the tank.

"Think that is the problem," Fynn said with a smile. "Try to start her now."

Rick turned the key and after a few turns of the starter motor, the engine burst into life.

"Well I'll be buggered," he exclaimed as Fynn was busy checking the breather hose.

"Reckon I have found the cause. Someone jammed a piece of wood against the tank and it has squashed the vent hose. That causes the tank to have a vacuum instead of venting."

"That was me," Rick relied. "It was the piece that held the old battery in position. When I put in a new bigger battery that bit of wood was no longer needed so I pushed it in alongside the tank just in case I ever need it again."

"Well done lad, you saved the day. Will catch up with you in Lincoln sometime, I owe you a coffee or a meal," Rick said as they again shook hands.

"Better call marine radio and let them know you are OK," suggested Fynn as he climbed back on to *Amethyst*. His attention was once again drawn towards Michelle who through the entire process had sat in the cabin to keep out of their way.

As the boats parted company Rick gave the thumbs up signal and waved. Michelle gave a petite hand wave that was clearly directed towards Fynn.

The afternoon breeze had strengthened to the forecasted 15 knots and filled *Amethyst*'s mainsail. Rick and Michelle who had since powered past and had disappeared into the distance heading towards Donnington. Fynn's mind was elsewhere as he mused about the girl he had momentarily met.

William had decide to go below take a nap as the yacht ran smoothly ahead of the wind. Helen stood near her son noting the distant look in his eyes.

"Nice looking lass eh?' she said to him.

"Who?" replied Fynn.

"Don't tell me you never noticed her. She is very pretty and looks to be quite at home on the sea. Perfect for you I say."

"She's OK I suppose," was Fynn's evasive answer.

"Maybe you should catch up with her. Girls like that are rare," Helen suggested as she turned to enter the cabin, leaving Fynn to his thoughts.

The following Saturday as Fynn was having *Amethyst* refueled by a local fuel agent, Rick accompanied by daughter Michelle strolled along the pontoon towards the yacht.

"Looks like you have visitors," the agent standing on deck called to Fynn who was down below busily checking the engine's oil level.

Fynn popped his head out of the engine room to see who his visitor might be.

"Came to thank you for your help last week," said Rick as he stepped from the pontoon, then held out his hand to shake Fynn's.

"They're a bit greasy – better wipe them first," Fynn stated as he climbed back on deck wiping his hands on a rag, before thrusting his hand out for the welcome shake with Rick, then turned toward Michelle saying "Hope you don't mind a bit of grease," holding out his hand to her, then without warning Michelle leaned forward and gave him a quick kiss on the cheek rather than the handshake.

"How about sharing a meal – your family and ours – my shout, as a reward for saving us," Rick smilingly proposed.

"When?" Fynn replied.

"Would next Friday night be too soon?" suggested Rick.

"Have to check with my parents first," answered Fynn, giving a quick sideways glance at Michelle.

"Here's my number. Give me a call soon," said Rick as he pulled a business card from his shirt pocket.

As father and daughter walked back along the pontoon towards the shore, Fynn's eyes were fixated on only one of the pair.

It was not until they were out of sight did he look down at the card he was holding that read 'Turner Development Company'.

"Michelle Turner!" Fynn muttered to himself.

That evening Helen rang Rick to thank him and accept the dinner invitation.

After a brief chat about the motor incident a time and place to meet was organised.

"Marina Hotel at seven o'clock Friday evening," Helen conveyed to William and Fynn who were busy watching television.

"There is time for you to get a haircut. That's if you want to impress Michelle," quipped William.

Fynn's eyes remained glued to the television and he said nothing.

For the ensuing days Helen busied herself each evening at the computer, downloading and printing her photos of the Osprey and the babies.

Normally Fynn would be full of interest and make comments on each of the many spectacular shots. Especially those of the outstretched talons as the bird was about to grab the fish.

Instead of being involve with the pictures, he went walking along the Parnkalla Trail to the Caravan Park and back, then occupied himself in the garage, sorting fishing tackle and cleaning the reels until it was time for bed.

While standing at the breakfast counter on Wednesday morning, William seriously asked Helen. "Am I imaging it or is Fynn behaving oddly?"

"Not at all. It is not unusual for a boy to be thinking of a girl, is it?" Helen replied, then winked.

"Ooohh. So that's what it is!" He chuckled and gave Helen a friendly squeeze on her curvaceous soft stern section.

"No time for that, we have to get to work. You too can think about it all day," Helen taunted.

A table for six on the deck over-looking the channel was reserved at the Hotel.

Both families arrived a several minutes prior to the appointed seven o'clock.

Helen and William dressed in neat casual clothes for the occasion. Fynn wore his faithful old denim jeans, Billabong windcheater and sandals.

His sun-blonded hair still had not yet met with the scissors.

The Turner family were attired in more formal clobber. Rick in suit-pants, coupled with a business shirt and tie.

His wife presented herself in an off the shoulder satin dress looking much like a magazine model, rather than a person on holiday.

Michelle wore a soft cotton loose floral printed dress and dainty sandals. Her long dark hair held back with a bejeweled butterfly clasp that sparkled under the overhead lighting.

As William and Rick greeted each other with a firm handshake, Helen reached out and gave Rick's wife a hug who then introduced herself as Maxine.

Fynn stood back momentarily unsure how to greet their daughter.

Michelle was more forward and quickly planted another of her unexpected kisses on Fynn's cheek causing a rush of reddening to his face.

Over their meal, stories of the marine adventures of both families were exchanged. The normally vocal Fynn sat subdued and did more listening than usual.

Rick however, predominantly held the floor in his boisterous salesman-like manner with tales of many game fishing exploits before giving a run-down on his business, being a property developer that specialised in setting up manufacturing areas and industrial estates.

Helen and Maxine engaged themselves in chats about their daily lives. Helen, the marine science worker, and Maxine, the (rather glamorous) stay-at-home and somewhat bored wife.

With both parents seemingly occupied in their own realms, Fynn bravely said to Michelle as he rose from his chair and tugged at her arm "Let's go sit around the other side that overlooks the yachts."

Without hesitation she rose from the table and followed Fynn through a sliding door to an outside lounge section of the waterfront deck.

A few minutes passed as they sat looking at the flotilla of leisure craft. Nervously Fynn began the conversation with "Your Dad gets excited doesn't he?"

Michelle gave a little giggle and said "He's always the salesman and keeps everyone's focus on him – but that is his profession. Your father sounds like he has an interesting career in the laboratory. That is what I would love to do when I finish school."

"He's is my Dad but not my Dad but I love him as being my Dad," confided Fynn, then lowered his head and said "My real father was also a Marine Scientist, but he died before I was born. Many years later, Mum married William and I now have a wonderful new Dad.'

"That's a spooky coincidence," Michelle replied as she slid her hand to rest gently on Fynn's. "Maxine is my stepmother and was once in the fashion industry. I call her dad's 'trophy wife'. When I was three my mother died suddenly, from a brain aneurism. I am not sure if Maxine loves Dad or if she is with him for a comfortable life-style. A nice house, her own car, a robe chock full of clothes and Dad's rich friends. Unfortunately I can't remember much about my mother except what I am told by Dad. He keeps some photos hidden away from Max. We sometimes look at them, mostly on Mum's birthday, the anniversary of the day they were married or when he is feeling melancholy. He still misses her. Every time he looks at her picture he says to me, "You are just a beautiful as your mother," Then we usually end up crying."

The emotion of her admission caused a tiny tear to trickle down Fynn's cheek.

Michelle reached out and with one finger gently wiped away his tear.

Taking a deep breath, Fynn then said as he took hold of her hand, "I can feel your pain. There was a time when I badly needed my Dad. An emptiness inside made me feel I had been cheated by not having a father. I believe it was fate that William became my father. He's a real good Dad and Mum always gave me heaps of love. William is madly in love with Mum."

Michelle moved closer to Fynn then rolled over her hand to entwine their fingers while she contemplated what to say next.

"I am not sure how much love Dad has for Maxine. Sadly, she doesn't like boats or the sea. We don't have much in common. Whereas Dad loves being on the water, and I do too. Some of his friends back in Sydney also have flash wives and big yachts or motor cruisers. We often go sailing with them. The boat we were on at the weekend – that broke down – is the one Dad keeps here in Lincoln in our holiday house garage." Michelle then paused for a brief second or two. "I can see you and your parents enjoys being together, I wish mine were that connected."

"Yep!" Replied Fynn, "That is the best thing about my Mum

and Dad, we do everything as a family."

The two sat holding hands while Fynn named most of the vessels (and their owners) that they could see berthed in that section of the marina. Then he pointed to the biggest one, a massive luxury power boat. "That one hardly gets used. Not like our *Amethyst*. We often take her out and go somewhere. Perhaps your family would like to come sailing with us next time?"

Just as Michelle was about to say 'Love to' the parents joined them. A slightly tipsy Rick, still holding a glass of red wine, loudly remarked while pointing to their entwined fingers with the glass, almost spilling its contents, "Looks like they have already made friends."

An embarrassed blush could be seen on both youngsters' faces.

After their 'connection' at the Marina Hotel dinner, Fynn was eager to see Michelle again. Fortunately they had exchanged phone numbers and were able to contact each other that night. Part way through their conversation Michelle said the words that dashed Fynn's hopes.

"Dad has an urgent business meeting on Tuesday. We are flying out early Sunday morning."

Adding further to his disappointment, her parents had arranged to meet some friends for lunch at the Mount Dutton Bay Wool Shed on Saturday afternoon.

"Can we catch up in the morning?" Fynn sheepishly asked.

"I wouldn't leave without seeing you again," Michelle reassured him.

Next morning, Michelle and her father arrived at the house.

While Helen and William involved themselves chatting with Rick about how delightful it was to meet and when the next time the Turners visit, a trip on *Amethyst* would be organised, Fynn and Michelle had wandered out into the front garden and stood close together gazing across the bay.

Without taking her eyes from the scenery Michelle's hand reached and touched Fynn's. His hand automatically clasped hers. "I'm going to miss you," she said.

Fynn gulped and nervously mumbled "Me too" and squeezed her hand gently.

The magic of the moment was suddenly broken by Rick. "Come on Missy, we have to pick up Maxine and head off to Dutton."

Michelle turned towards Fynn and gave him another of her impromptu kisses – but this time, on his lips.

Fynn stood like a stunned statue as the Turners began to drive off. "Bye, phone me tonight!" Michelle called and waved her arm out of the car window.

Discreetly William nudged Helen and whispered to her, "His first love."

Fynn's persona had been transformed since first sighting Michelle on the Turner's broken down boat. His focus was no longer concentrating on fishing and sailing. Fynn was smitten by the young lass.

Several times during the afternoon he tried phoning Michelle, each time receiving the same automated message, *'The number you are calling is either switched off or out of range, please try again later'.*

Unbeknown to him, Michelle was also trying to phone his number and without success. Her mobile phone was serviced by a company that did not have coverage in that area.

With regular failed attempts to contact her, the afternoon hours dragged by for Fynn who languished on his bed staring at the ceiling.

That evening when contact was re-established Fynn's spirit lifted. His usual smile broadened as his happiness level rose.

Excitedly, Michelle and Fynn chatted for two hours until Rick intervened and demanded Michelle, 'get off the phone and get some sleep – we have an early start in the morning'.

As soon as he awakened next morning, Fynn checked his phone. There was a text message waiting that simply said. 'Love you, miss you. x x'.

Immediately Fynn tried to return a call. Once again that disheartening recorded message was received. *'The number you are calling…'*

At the breakfast table a dejected lad sat staring at his bowl of cereal.

Noting Fynn's glum mood, William coerced him to help with a cleanup of *Amethyst's* cabins. Fynn reluctantly followed Will onto the boat whilst repeatedly checking his phone.

Apart from receiving two annoying scam-calls, both informing him that his computer has a virus, and despite his many attempts to contact Michelle plus multiple texts sent, Fynn heard nothing more.

Now the question on Fynn's mind 'Why won't she return my calls and texts?'

Young love has the power to turn a happy-chappy to a moping-misery. This was the obvious case with the teenager whose only focus, before meeting Michelle, was to be on the water.

With a heavy heart Fynn dragged himself through the following days.

At the Marine Science Centre, Will received an unexpected phone call.

On the phone was a somewhat agitated Michelle who explained that her family was now in Sydney and her phone had fallen from her pocket into the Harbour on the first day of a three day cruise whilst boating with her father's friends.

Michelle hurriedly explained how neither parent had any contact details for Fynn's family. The only number was on her phone, and that was now swimming with the fishes.

"Can you give me Fynn's number," she almost begged.

Fynn lay on his bed with eyes closed, lost in his misery of why Michelle had dumped him.

Never before had he experienced such a feeling of loss.

Being forgiving by nature, his thoughts gradually transferred from his situation, to a realisation of the pain his mother would have felt when his father died.

His mind floated into trying to picture how life would have been if his father was still alive.

Suddenly he was snapped back to reality when his phone began to ring. Thinking it was mother checking, he lazily picked it up – an unrecognised number illuminated on the screen.

Thinking it was another nuisance scammer or seller, Fynn pressed the hang-up button and placed the phone back on the bedside table.

Again the phone rang. "Whatever ya selling – I don't want one!" The irritate Fynn loudly told the caller.

"Fynn, it's me – Michelle – don't hang up!"

Michelle related her story of accidently dropping the phone overboard and how she had tried to contact him. It was her father's suggestion to phone William at the Science Centre to get his number.

A much relieved Fynn confessed that he thought she had lost interest in furthering their relationship.

"Fynn, the very first time I saw you..." she began, then came a moment of awkward silence. Michelle timidly continued, 'Fynn, Do you believe on love at first sight? I fell for you when we first met. How could I ever lose interest in you?"

"Scary stuff isn't it," Fynn said softly into his phone. "I haven't thought of anything else since I saw you out at the reef. Never given any time to thinking about girls. Until I met you life had always the sea and boats!"

"When are you coming back to Lincoln?" Fynn enquired, anticipating it may be many months before they see each other again.

"That is why I have been trying so hard to get in touch. We will be there next week," Michelle announced with a girlish giggle.

Michelle's new number was now logged into his contacts and each night they chatted for at least an hour.

Even with daily contact, having to wait a week had Fynn torn between excitement and impatience.

Helen had noted his anxiety and suggested he burn off his energy putting time into the garden, mowing and trimming shrubs.

"Never seen him work that hard," William said to Helen as they watched him through the kitchen window.

"He is so excited that Michelle is coming – young love is powerful emotion," she replied.

"I reckon Fynn is turning from a boy to a man. He has finally noticed there are girls in the world," Will responded then politely reminded his wife, "Don't forget – we promised the Turner's a trip on *Amethyst*. A trip to Spilsby Island and back would be nice."

The Turner family had arrived back in Lincoln and a time was set for the Spilsby trip on the weekend.

Unfortunately on the arranged morning, a larger than the average swell for the entire day, was forecast by the weather bureau.

"Instead of having an uncomfortable sail out to Spilsby today, how about we settle for trip around the bay. We can drop anchor out from Peter's homestead on Boston Island and do a bit of fishing," William suggested.

"And then,"... chimed in Helen. "We can have an evening dinner of fresh fish. That's if we catch any."

William quickly responded. "But just to be sure – How about getting some fresh Spencer Gulf prawns before we go, and cook them up, just to show Rick that we have the best prawns in Australia – right here in Port Lincoln."

"Brilliant idea" said Helen.

It was only Rick (with several bottle of red wine tucked under his arm), and Michelle that strolled down the pontoon. As anticipated, Maxine was a 'no-show' for the day out. Her excuse was 'she could feel a headache coming on'!

At start of the trip, (to show-off his boating skills to Michelle), Fynn took command and motored *Amethyst* out of the marina, then, when clear of the channel beacon, set about raising the jib then the main sail.

"You can take over now," he said to William, who was already at the helm steering the boat while Fynn was up forward.

Fynn took Michelle's hand and guided to the bow. There they sat, until they reached the Island.

One each side of the vessels bowsprit, with their legs dangling over the hull, and engaged themselves in deep conversation, interspersed occasionally with a giggle from Michelle whenever a dolphin swam near the boat.

"Never seen my daughter so happy. They seem well suited to each other," remarked Rick.

"Yep and the same goes for Fynn. The last time I saw him with such a big smile is when he was given his first real boat – Nautical Buoy," said Helen.

At the Island, Fynn and Michelle sat on the foredeck and continued their chatting and let the parents do the fishing. Unfortunately, the fishing was unproductive.

One purple leather jacket, two small flat head and one undersized whiting.

"Prawns it is then," Helen reminded William who was trying without success to jag a very timid squid.

Rick had already seen the bottom of the bottle of one of the red wines as Helen served the meal of crumbed prawns and salads.

To be social with their guest, William had drunk only one can of beer before the meal, while Helen was content with soft drink.

Being down in the cabin the group did not see the sun creep behind the hills. At the table their conversations drifted from Rick's latest business venture to perhaps coming to live in Port Lincoln on a permanent basis. For Fynn and Michelle, these were magic words.

"Well there goes another one," Rick slurred as he drained the last drop of wine from his second bottle.

"Time to clean up and head home," Helen suggested as she collected plates and cutlery from the table.

William was first on deck, "Black as a dogs out here," he remarked as his eyes adjusted to the darkness.

Rick and two young ones followed him out of the bright cabin lights.

"As soon as your mother finishes cleaning up we will get underway. It's calm and not any wind so we won't need a sail – we will just motor home," William said to Fynn.

"Right O, Captain," Fynn cheekily answered.

Amethyst sliced through the dark glassy water. Reflections of the Port and Starboard lights shone red and green on the surface as they traveled. In the distance the lights of Lincoln also created a kaleidoscope of colour on the mirror like surface.

Everyone eyes were focused on the illuminations. Rick went to move closer to the cabin when *Amethyst* gave an unexpected lurch as a bow wave from another vessel hit.

To save himself from tripping over, his outstretched his arm accidently knocked Michelle forward making her unbalanced. Then *Amethyst* lurched again, sending Rick sprawling on the deck and his daughter over the side into the water.

Fynn and his mother had been in this situation on a previous occasion when William accidently took a swim.

William grabbed the spotlight and shone towards where Michelle had fallen. He moved the light back and forth without sighting her.

"Michelle. Michelle," screamed Fynn as Helen stopped the boat where she had been.

Fynn ripped of his shirt and dived into the ink-black water. Furious he swam around calling her name while William scanned back and forth with the light.

On deck Rick was sobbing how sorry he was. Helen remained calm and held the boat in position while William, kept searching with the light.

They could hear Fynn frantically calling, "Please God – where is she, don't let her die!' Then, he did another dive down into the blackness.

Fynn surfaced again almost crying, "Mum I can't see a thing, it is too black down there," looked around then in desperation dived back under.

It had been nearly three minutes since Michelle tumbled over the rail.

Fear gripped at Rick's throat as he blubbered "I'm sorry – I'm sorry my darling – I'm sorry."

Suddenly, Fynn exploded, gasping for breath through the surface about fifteen metres away from the boat. William swung the light towards him then yelled,

"Rick – look, he's got Michelle!"

Fynn had one arm holding the dorsal fin of a very familiar dolphin and the other wrapped around a spluttering Michelle's shoulders. The dolphin was dragging both towards the yacht.

After Michelle's near limp body was hoisted onto the deck, she began coughing and vomiting sea water. In the meantime Helen was alerting medical authorities on her mobile phone.

An exhausted Fynn with tear filled eyes sat next to Michelle, reassuring her that everything was going to be alright.

The shock and the adrenalin rush had made Rick somewhat more sober. However, his tears continued as the gravity of the situation fully dawned on him.

As *Amethyst* pulled alongside the town jetty, they were met by two paramedics and a policeman.

Michelle was transferred from the vessel, then taken to the emergency ward of the hospital. Rick accompanied his daughter in the ambulance.

Having no transport, a distraught Fynn begged the attending policeman to take him and follow the medics.

"I am not supposed to give rides – but his time I will, as I need to get a statement from you. Might as well do it at the hospital," he said with a wink.

Helen and William then motored *Amethyst* back to the marina pontoon and secured the boat.

They too drove to the hospital in William's car that they had left parked at the marina prior to the outing.

Word had been sent to Maxine of the incident, and she too hurried to the hospital.

Both families sat nervously in the waiting room for news of Michelle's wellbeing.

Over an hour had passed since Rick arrived in the ambulance.

Then a Doctor approached the group. "Which of you is the girl's father," he enquired looking first at William.

"I am," Rick replied as he thrust out his hand for his habitual salesman style greeting. This was ignored by the doctor.

Then in a serious tone, "The good news is, your daughter is doing as well as can be expected. However secondary drowning is not out of the question when water has entered the lungs. Because your daughter had some water in her lungs it will be necessary for her to stay in hospital for at least the next 24 hours to monitor her condition."

"When can we see her?" a much relieved Rick and Fynn asked in unexpected unison.

"I will inform the nurse that Michelle has visitors and she will let you know when you may see her." The doctor said, then walked back down the corridor.

Propped up with pillows, Michelle looked bedraggled. Her hair was tangle and her completion was pale.

"Looks like she could do with a makeover,' Maxine snobbishly remarked as they entered the room.

"I have seen you look worse than that Max," nervously chortled Rick in an attempt to hide his relief that his daughter was still alive.

"She still looks beautiful to me," Fynn said as he approached the bed, then leaned forward and kissed Michelle's forehead.

"You saved me. I thought that a shark was going to eat me." Michelle said as she reached out and held Fynn's hand.

"No, it wasn't a shark," he replied.

Then Michelle said with a questioning look, "The water was black as night, I didn't know which way was up and could not see anything. I could feel something big was trying to bite me and I kept pushing it away. I was so frightened and running out of breath. I thought I was going to die."

"That same 'something' as you call it, pushed me towards you. It was 'Splash' a crazy dolphin that follows me around the bay. Without him, I never would have found you. I managed to grab you and then his dorsal fin. Then he hauled us both up to the surface."

"It's true," William said, then added "In the spotlight I saw Fynn holding onto Splash who was dragging you both towards the boat."

"Really! So it wasn't a shark," said the much relieved young lady.

The next evening, after having been checked and cleared by the doctor, Michelle was allowed to leave hospital.

Within a few days the effects of the near drowning had dissipated and Michelle was able to spend time with Fynn exploring the hidden gems of Port Lincoln.

The events of that near tragic night had given Rick Turner a wake-up shake. He needed someone to talk with.

Most of his acquaintances were what he described as 'high rollers' and seemed to lack the wisdom of good parenting. A few of them had sent their children off to boarding at elite schools in anticipation they would make connections with other wealthy families.

Rick realised that he had become that type of person. Like his associates he too was involved in business deals and utilizing the system for his own advantage with the single aim, to make more money.

Almost losing his daughter, Rick now recognised that he needed to change his ways. He had gathered much wealth over the years but no amount of money would have bought her back if she had not been saved. 'What good is money if one is not happy?' He mused while reflecting on his own endeavors to accumulate more wealth.

At work in the lab, William received a text message that simply said 'Mate, I need to talk with someone. Can we meet up for coffee or lunch? – Rick'

Rather than text his reply William phoned back.

"Got your message – are you OK," a concerned William asked.

"Yeh sort of," Rick replied. "I need a good listener. Almost losing my daughter and have had already lost her mother I am a bloody wreck," he confessed.

Sensing Rick was low in spirit William suggested. "I'll take the rest of the day off and we can meet up somewhere. What say I grab something to eat and we lunch onboard *Amethyst*? No crowd to contend with. Is that good for you? I can be there in about an hour!"

"Thanks mate, see you in an hour," Rick quietly replied.
In the solitude of *Amethyst*'s cabin a teary Rick explained that he had gone through hell when his wife had died. The magnitude of almost losing Michelle had shaken him to a point where he now realised that he should change his lifestyle.

Rick's eyes began to fill with tears, "You know, it was me that accidently pushed her over the rail. I was too drunk to stand. Got to give up the wine before something else happens. Not only would I have lost Michelle I would have broken Fynn's heart." He wiped away tears that now flowed freely down his cheeks.

"I had not seen it that way – Fynn would have been devastated. I was just concerned that your daughter was safe," said William as he exhaled heavily as he passed a box of tissues to Rick.

Both men sat in silence. Each in their own thoughts reliving the near tragedy.

Rick was first to speak. "Time for me to get out of the business rat-race. Start a new life and do something different. Sell up my other houses and live here Lincoln. What do you think?" he said with a new-found confidence.

"Helen and I have never been keen on big-city life. We are happy here and Fynn is in his element. He has the water, the boats and we have each other. The big question is – What would Maxine think of your plan?"

"Inside that posh model exterior is another person. I believe Max would love to wipe off the makeup and bung on a pair of old jeans and get her hands dirty," revealed Rick. "I have seen how she watches other women having carefree fun. I think Max has been trapped in the model mode for too long. Almost certain she is tired of always having to look her best. A bit of country living on a small acreage would do her good – and me as well."

"Would you mind if I organise a shin-dig for us all. To celebrate the Turner's making Port Lincoln their new home. Where do you recommend?"

"If you're paying? I have heard some great reports of a place that has its own vineyards," suggested William relieved that Rick had seemingly overcome his earlier sadness.

"Sounds good – Leave the arrangements to me," said a much happier Rick who now had the burden he was carrying lifted from his shoulders. "Has anybody told you that are a good man William Scott? Thank you for caring." Rick smiled as he reached out and firmly shook Wills hand.

"That is what mateship is all about. Being considerate and kind to each other. I sensed you were hurting. If I can do more – just ask," William replied.

Autumn drifted into winter. The chill of the southerly winds made being on the water an uncomfortable experience. Days of rain and wind kept the Scott's inside. Their life in the family household was centred on reading books and magazines while listening to music in the cosy warmth of the open-fired lounge room. Towards the latter half of August a notable desire to get outdoors again was obvious.

An absence of wind, calm seas and some much welcome sunshine arrived in early September. That type of day provided a great an opportunity to go fishing.

Being blessed with a day that was in stark contrast to the chilly Port Lincoln winter weather, Fynn and Dad William decided to seize the opportunity and give *Nautical Buoy* a run. They hoped to replenish the freezer with calamari and whatever else their baits would attract.

As they prepared to launched their boat from Billy Lights Point boat ramp they met with Tony, a rather jovial ex-profession fisherman, who was also taking advantage of the lull in the rough weather and was ready to launch his boat and head off fishing.

"Where do you reckon would be the best place to get a good feed today?" Fynn asked.

Being guarded about his favourite locations, Tony suggested "Behind Boston Island." Then added "Try the white holes out from Picnic Beach. If there're no whiting – you could catch some decent size squid."

Tony's boat was first away from the pontoon and he headed towards Fanny Point. William and Fynn followed a few minutes later. Both boats skimmed smoothly across the bay on the glass-calm water. When *Nautical Buoy* rounded Fanny Point they noticed that Tony was veering more towards the

Donington Lighthouse.

"He did say Picnic Beach didn't he?" William asked Fynn.

"Reckon the sneaky old bugger might have told us a fib," Fynn replied then added. "Might as well try there, just in case he wasn't."

When *Nautical Buoy* passed Rotten Bay they could see that Tony had no intention of fishing behind the island. He had rounded Donington Lighthouse and was now heading south towards Carcase Rock.

Out from Picnic Beach the water was deep and crystal clear. Finding a white-hole along the weed-line to fish was easy. Both men soon had their lines baited and in the water.

The instant Fynn's line hit the sandy bottom he got a bite, but missed the hook-up. "Bugger! Wasn't expecting that," he moaned as he retrieved his line to rebait. Next it was William's turn to get a bite.

"Got ya," he called out as he pulled in a nice legal length whiting. Within a minute Fynn was also landing his first fish, another good size King George. After bagging another six fish the biting stopped.

"I reckon it's time to shift to another patch," suggested Fynn as he placed his rod in the holder.

"Agree with that," William said as he wound in his line.

As he pressed the anchor winch button Fynn looked around for his next location. Then he noticed Tony's boat headed towards them. "Looks like the old bugger has had a change of mind – he's headed this way. Don't tell him we've already got a feed," Fynn said.

"Hey, have you blokes got the Fisheries phone number," Tony anxiously called as he pulled alongside.

"Yes, it's on my phone," William answered.

"Give them a call will ya? – there's a whale coming this way dragging a heap of rope tangled around its tail," explained Tony.

"I'll dial it and you can speak to them," William said, then passed his phone over to Tony who was now holding his boat alongside.

"G'day – is that the Fisheries?" Tony almost yelled into the phone then listened for the reply.

"Got a whale out here that needs help. It's tail is tangled in masses of rope and there're a couple of floats dragging behind it. I reckon it is heading towards the back of Boston Island."

Once again he paused for a few seconds as he listened then continued the conversation.

"Yeah OK, we'll stay with it and keep you up to date with it's location. How long will it take ya to get here?" he asked, then blurted "Two hours – the bloody thing could be at Louth Bay by then." Another pause and he replied. "OK, we'll keep a watch on it for youse. We have two boats here, so that will make it easier for ya to spot. Might pay to come out the North entrance. That might save a heap of time cos the whale is moving that way. OK, thanks, see ya."

He passed the phone back to William.

"Where is it now?" Fynn asked.

"Probably just goin' past September Beach. Two bloody hours..." a frustrated Tony growled.

The two craft headed towards where the whale was last seen. The huge creature was making slow progress and had not yet passed the beach area.

'It's a young Right Whale and it seems to be stressed. Poor

thing," Fynn said as they idled the boat near the laboriously swimming creature.

"That's not just rope. It is a heap of old long-line from off a foreign fishing boat. Still got some hooks attached," said William, while Fynn manoeuvred the boat as close as he could.

"Those big floats a causing a heap of drag – no wonder it's difficult to make any headway," yelled Tony as he too positioned his craft a safe distance from the struggling whale.

"Two hours is too long. I reckon I could jump in and cut the rope near the tail," Fynn suggested to William.

"Nah – too dangerous," replied Will.

"He's hardly moving forward against the outgoing tide. Soon it will be going backwards if the rip gets any stronger," Fynn stated.

"See how much those floats are slowing it down? Maybe if you just cut the rope behind the whale, it would give it a chance," said William with a tad of reluctance to allow Fynn to enter the water.

Not waiting for Will to change his mind Fynn stripped off his tops, slipped on a pair of flippers grabbed from the under-seat storage locker and went over the side with a sharp fishing-knife in hand. The immense power of the outflowing water caught him by surprise and made it difficult for Fynn to swim alongside the creature. But, being a strong swimmer Fynn was finally able to grab hold of some rope just behind the tail fluke.

His added weight to the lines momentarily panicked the whale and it reacted by diving deeper, taking the lad with him. Fynn's lungs were near bursting when the whale finally resurfaced.

Avoiding the movement of each tail stroke Fynn cut at the mass of entangle cordage. Only on the up-stroke of the tail, could Fynn use the knife. Every down thrust caused the whale to drag Fynn under, thus forcing him to hang on and hold his breath until the tail came near the surface once again. Eight minutes of hacking at the ropes had passed without freeing the whale from its burden of discarded marine debris.

Fynn finally realised why some of the ropes remained tightly wrapped around the unfortunate mammal's tail. A large hook had become embedded in the forward edge of the fluke. In his effort to hang on and stay with the whale, he was unable to release the offending hook.

He struggled for several minutes to sever the wire trace that held the hook to the mainline but his knife could not cut through the stainless wires. The only hope he had was to keep hacking away at another section of ropes that were still wrapped around where big mammal's tail and body met.

His arms were tiring and holding his breath was becoming more arduous. He would soon have to give up his rescue attempt. With one last super effort, he plunged his knife between several tightly packed ropes. Then let the current drag him backward to increase the pressure to the blade. Miraculously, the knife cut through two of the offending cords.

Sensing a lessening of the constriction the whale flicked its huge tail out of the water. The remaining sections of rope parted and finally freed the creature.

Without thought of the consequences Fynn still clung to a piece of the mainline rope. The trailing floats were now being propelled away from the whale by the fast-flowing out-running tide. Fynn felt a sharp pain in his thigh. A hook on a wire trace had embedded itself into his leg.

"Arrgh," he yelped as the hook plunged itself deeper into his flesh. Blood spurted from the wound.

William had been observing the procedure, and when he heard Fynn's cry and saw the blood-stained water he manoeuvred the boat to travel in unison with the floats and the now-hooked Fynn. Reaching over with a gaff, he lifted a section of line out of the water. In agony, Fynn managed to knife through the offending cordage and release himself – the hook still embedded deep in his thigh.

"Grab the gaff shaft and I'll pull you aboard," William shouted.

As he strained, fighting the current to bring the lad to the boat, he suddenly spotted movement in the water.

"Shark!!"

Throughout the episode Fynn had remained calm and in control. But his blood had attracted a large shark that had probably been shadowing the whale, waiting for an opportunity to feed on its blubber.

A weakened Fynn somehow managed to maintain his grip on the shaft. In contrast, William's adrenalin surge empowered him far beyond his normal strength. With only seconds to spare he dragged Fynn against the flowing current to the boat.

The shark charged at them with mouth wide open, exposing it's jaw full of flesh-carving razor-sharp teeth.

Will miraculously lifted Fynn clear and onto the stern just before the shark reached them. It rolled onto its side, scraping it's teeth along the hull before disappearing into the depths.

Now laying on the floor of the boat Fynn passed out and was rapidly losing blood.

Will hastily fashioned a tourniquet from a short piece of mooring rope and applied pressure to the upper leg. The First-Aid course he had taken months earlier now had purpose. His quick action stemmed the blood loss.

From his boat, Anthony saw the bloodied water and Fynn's predicament. Acting instinctively, he dialled triple zero on his phone and alerted a paramedic crew.

"Go to Snapper Rock," he shouted across to William. "Your boat is faster than mine. An ambulance will meet you there. I'll explain to the Fisheries what happened and will catch up with you later."

"Don't panic – don't panic," William said to himself as he pushed the throttle down as hard as he could on *Nautical Buoy* and pointed the craft towards Lincoln.

Albeit for the tide-flow lumpy section between the lighthouse and Donington Island, the sea had remained calm.

Nautical Buoy skimmed flat out, and fortunately for Fynn, sped smoothly across the bay.

Fynn's eyes began to gradually open. Groggily he asked, "Where are we, Dad?"

"Heading for Snapper Rock – an ambulance will meet us there. Just a few minutes more. Hang in there. You're going to be alright. I love you, son."

Fynn softly responded, "Love you too, Dad," then lapsed again into unconsciousness.

While speeding across the bay William had phoned Helen and told her of the incident.

She was waiting anxiously with the paramedics watching the boat as it neared Snapper Rock.

Now was not the time to be concerned about any hull damage, so William ran the fibreglass *Nautical Buoy* straight up onto the smooth sloping granite rock.

Without hesitation one of the paramedics jumped aboard to

attend to Fynn. Firstly with oxygen, then inserting a drip in his arm before they rushed him away in the ambulance.

Helen went with him to the hospital.

As the ambulance pulled away Will's adrenalin rush came to an abrupt end. Now unable to control his emotions, he sat on the huge slab of the ancient rock and bawled.

A couple of local blokes consoled William until he regained his composure. Knowing that William and Helen lived not far away they volunteered to take the boat back to Billy Light's and return both car and boat to the house. One chap that had his car parked nearby offered to either take William home or to the hospital.

Will opted to be dropped off at the house. He managed to joke that the hospital may not let him enter, as he was wearing his fishing clothes that smelled of bait and were now blood-soaked as well.

After having a quick shower and donning fresh clothes he drove himself to the hospital in Helen's car. He was met by a very concerned Turner family who somehow had been given the news of Fynn's plight.

A visibly upset Helen was talking privately with the surgeon. He explained that Fynn's life was saved by William's tourniquet. However, Fynn required an immediate operation to repair his thigh where the hook had ripped through the muscle. After that, he should be off the danger list.

A relieved Helen relayed the part about the needed surgery to William and the Turners, explaining that Fynn would need to stay in hospital for several days – to monitor his well-being and ensure there was no infection and to allow the internal stitches to hold."

Before Helen had finished, a nervously anxious Michelle interrupted, "When can we see him?"

Helen clarified that he was still in theatre and they could all see him in the morning.

Back at the Scott household, Helen looked William in the eye. "The doctor said you saved his life." She hugged him tight. As she released herself, she held up a finger which she pointed at Will. "You have got some explaining to do Mister Scott – what happened?"

The events of the day were described in detail.

"All I can say is that Fynn will always be saving someone or something. That's in his nature. There's no way can we stop that."

For the first time in his life Fynn had been seriously injured. He now carried fifteen stitches in his leg.

Michelle fussed over her injured 'hero'.

The bond between William and Fynn was stronger than ever. William's only remark was "Let's not do anything like that again. I'd hate to face what would have happened if that shark had got there a few seconds earlier. Just thinking about it sends shivers down my spine."

This had been a timely reminder that no one is bullet-proof, as his father had discovered.

As Fynn began to mend Rick fulfilled his promise to organise a gathering. The date and time for the 'party' was marked on the calendar.

"Quite a busy place," said Rick as the families walked into the restaurant foyer.

"One of Lincoln's best kept secrets," William said with a grin.

As they entered Fynn caught a glimpse of someone who seemed familiar. "Will – isn't that the boy we saved, sitting over there?" he asked as he pointed discreetly in the lad's direction.

"I reckon it is," William replied.

Before anything further could be said, or answers given, they were interrupted by a polite young hostess.

"Good evening Mr Turner, welcome to our restaurant. The table for your party is this way." She gestured for them to follow.

After allowing the group to peruse the menu, the well-trained staff began to take their orders. Fynn then lifted his eyes away from the enticing desert section and looked around the room.

"Mum, that's' the blokes from Reevesby Island, and isn't that the little girl and her mother from Shelley Beach?"

Unbeknown to the Scotts, Rick Turner had secretly invited several other guests.

"What's going on?" enquired Fynn looking at his mother.

His eyes surveyed the other diners. Among the crowd were more familiar people.

Old family friends, had also been invited – Julie and Peter and their daughter Saffron, Kerry, James, Doctor Ian and the vet Roger.

"Ladies and gentlemen," announced Rick as he rose to his feet and tapped the side of a wine glass with a spoon to attract everyone's attention.

Then he began to speak in a rather formal voice of an MC.

"Thank you all for coming. Firstly let me explain. Not many here would know us, the Turner family, as we are not yet locals. However we have been holidaying in this area for several years and have been impressed with the natural beauty and the friendliness of the people.

"Now we wish to make this lovely place our home, and be part of your community." Then with a chuckle quipped "That's if you will have me!"

Rick continued his speech. "A recent incident brought me to realise that there are times in one's life when, through unknown forces, total strangers meet. These meeting can change the course of your life. My family have been part of that phenomenon."

Rick held out one arm with his palm open in the direction of Helen and William.

"I am sure they need no introduction – once strangers, now our friends the Scotts," he said as he clapped his hands together.

All those present in the room – staff and guests – also applauded.

William spontaneously put his arm around Helen and drew her closer to his side and kissed her cheek.

Rick then continued, "Having spent quite some time to track all of you down, I have another reason for bringing everyone together. This evening, is not just about my family wanting to make Port Lincoln our new home. It is also to sincerely thank an amazing young man who saved my daughter, and many others of you in this room."

Then he walked over to Fynn who had already risen to his feet and was now standing beside his parents.

Rick went to thrust out his arm in his usual way to do a business style handshake, instead he lifted his other arm, then gave Fynn an embracing man-hug.

"Fynn – you are an extraordinary young fellow. Maxine,

Michelle and I will never forget how you have come to our rescue on two occasions. From the stories that I have heard, you are continually helping save other people. Apart from you, there has also been another element to some of your rescues. There seems to be the attraction that a certain dolphin has to you. It is amazing how this one dolphin has singled you out to be his friend. I would not be surprised if somewhere there is a higher influence involved in your life."

As soon as Rick had said that, Helen reached out and squeezed Fynn's hand, smiled and softly said to him 'Mark'.

Summer time on Eyre Peninsula! Another glorious mid-January Mediterranean type of day on Boston Harbour! The temperature hovered around a balmy 32 degrees. The enticing turquoise water of the bay bustled with activity – yachting, paddle-boarding and swimming.

Fynn and Michelle were swimming about eighty metres out from Shelly Beach.

Suddenly a dark shape from below began to circle them.

Michelle started to panic. "Shark!" she yelled and grabbed a tight hold of Fynn.

He laughed and reassured her. "No, it's not a shark – It's just my cheeky mate 'Splash'."

* 9 7 8 0 6 4 8 8 9 7 0 3 3 *